M000092077

# My Big Apartment

Mon grand appartement

by Christian Oster

Translated & with an introduction by Jordan Stump

UNIVERSITY OF NEBRASKA PRESS : LINCOLN & LONDON

Original title: Mon grand appartement ©
1999 by Éditions de Minuit. Translation &
introduction © 2002 by the University of
Nebraska Press. All rights reserved. Manu-
factured in the United States of America ⊛
Publication of this translation was assisted
by a grant from the French Ministry of
Culture – National Center for the Book.

Library of Congress Cataloging-in-Publication Data
Oster, Christian.
[Mon grand appartement. English.]
My big apartment = Mon grand appartement /
Christian Oster ; translated and with an introduction
by Jordan Stump.
p. cm.
ISBN 0-8032-3567-4 (cloth : alkaline paper) –
ISBN 0-8032-8612-0 (paperback : alkaline paper)
I. Title: Mon grand appartement. II. Stump, Jordan,
1959– III. Title.
PQ2675.S698 M66 2002  843'.914-dc21   2002017977

# Translator's Introduction

A French reviewer of *My Big Apartment* writes that its plot could fit comfortably onto a Post-it note. This may well be true; the novel's story (a man with a big apartment eventually finds a bigger one, we might say) does have a certain slightness about it, but beyond that lies something wonderfully rich, intricate, and various. Complexity behind simplicity: such might be the rule of Christian Oster's writing, a rule incarnated, first of all, in his own career. He is the author of eight novels stamped with the mark of one of France's most adventurous publishing houses, the Éditions de Minuit, but he has also written a number of pseudonymous detective novels and even a handful of darkly funny children's books. His writing might at any given moment be classified as minimalist or baroque, postmodern or sentimental, comic or tragic, or both, or neither. If his books have a message to transmit, he has said, it must be something like "let's go on living all the same" – scarcely a message at all, in other words, behind which, once again, nevertheless lies a whole world of hope, disappointment, despair, and revival.

A few common threads – deceptively simple, here too – unite Oster's Minuit novels. They are without exception love stories: stories of the difficulties of love, its unattainability, its travails, sometimes even its triumphs. His protagonists tend to be no-longer-quite-young men, bruised and disappointed in their sentiments but forever hopeful, with their hearts prominently and vulnerably displayed on their sleeves. There is a palpable sadness to the lives these men lead, a sort of melancholy even in their happiest moments, an offhand but insistent awareness of the fragility of every pleasure. Hence, perhaps, their exaggerated sensitivity to life's smaller difficulties, unarmed as they are before the thousand minor obstacles with which the physical world confronts us every day. Hence too, I think, the oddly self-conscious nature of their language: Oster's narrators are sincere to a fault, but they do not seem to be able to say anything *simply*. Perhaps the web of their feelings is too tangled for easy expression; perhaps language simply eludes their control, like every other aspect of their lives. For whatever reason, their speech is the opposite of straightforward, and in this lies another crucial component of Oster's writing: its tremendous humor, at once discreet, outlandish, smart, and quietly melancholy. Complex, as well, for although Oster's novels can make us laugh out loud, he is not exactly a comic writer; similarly, although there is a great sadness in his stories, his vision seems to me the very opposite of tragic. We cannot even say that his protagonists lead lives of quiet desperation – only perpetual disappointment, and a sort of resignation, and an enduring hope that the next time they will get it right, and a deeply ingrained sense that they probably won't.

Such is indeed the lot of Gavarine, the narrator of *My Big Apartment*. But I do not mean to suggest that this seventh of Oster's eight novels merely recycles the preoccupations of its predecessors. Quite the reverse: he has a remarkable gift for recasting his characters' struggles in perpetually fresh form and for offering the reader new and delightful surprises with every novel. It was no doubt this inventiveness that earned *My Big Apartment* one of France's most prestigious literary prizes on its publication in 1999: the Prix Médicis, intended for works of particular originality by writers less celebrated than their talent deserves. The bestowal of the Médicis on *My Big Apartment* is high praise indeed, and were this novel nothing more than a wry romantic comedy, the choice might well seem incongruous. It *is* a wry romantic comedy, of course, but not *only* that. Its charms are at once unapologetically sentimental and overtly intellectual, for Oster's writing belongs to that particularly noble strain of French literature in which seriousness and jest, or passion and the cerebral, fruitfully coexist without effort or contradiction. Think of Queneau in the first case and Colette in the second; such (among many others) are Oster's antecedents, and like theirs, his novels cannot be defined in one simple term but blithely tell one story even as they tell another.

*My Big Apartment* is in one sense the tale of a man who loses his keys and then finds them again; it is also the story of a man who grows up, gradually learning to forget his self-absorption; or again, it is a paean to the redemptive qualities of love or something like it. There is always more going on here than meets the eye, and nothing is ever simple: not the keys, not the narrator's self-absorption, and certainly not the love story. Not the novel's ingenious structure, either, which is once again of an oddly dual nature. As this strange tale winds from Paris to south-central France on its way toward an ending that manages to be both happy and ambiguous, everything seems to happen spontaneously, as if by accident; this aimless or uncontrolled quality is real and irrefutable, but no less real is the novel's wonderfully subtle (and typically Osterian) symmetry. For, no matter how it might seem, this is a very carefully controlled book (again, one thinks of Queneau): look closely, and you will find that its story echoes itself in the most curious and suggestive ways, with certain images or even mere turns of phrase discreetly recurring at unexpected moments and incidents from the beginning troublingly reproduced, albeit in a distorted or transmuted form, in the end. I prefer not to give examples here – to do so would spoil some of the novel's nicest surprises – but I do think it important to alert the reader to this further example of the complexity of Oster's approach: the novel is *at the same time* aimless and structured, irreducibly and, more astonishing yet, meaningfully.

The same might be said, as the reader will soon discover, of Gavarine's idiosyncratic narrative voice. The tale he wants to tell us might seem relatively slight, as that French reviewer's hyperbolic quip suggests, but the manner in which he tells it is remarkably lush. By this I mean not only that he tends to consider the implications of anodyne events in exhaustive detail but also that his language is one unfailingly rich in implications; here too, there is more than meets the eye. Gavarine has a fondness, conscious or unconscious, for utterances with a double meaning – not puns exactly but words or phrases that say two things at once, connoting far more than they dare to express. And this insistence on the unspoken is not his only game with language: he has a similar penchant for playing with the reader's expectations, forever leading us to believe that a given sentence is going in one direction when in fact it is headed in quite another, or (exploiting the relative leniency of the rules governing dialogue punctuation in French) that a given utterance is spoken by a character when it is in fact spoken by the narrator, or vice versa. It can be dizzying, struggling to keep up with a narrator whose speech so frequently lags behind or ahead of his thoughts, but the result is a pleasant sort of disorientation and never a gratuitous one. Gavarine does not always tell us what we need to know, nor speak in the form we might prefer; somehow, though, through all his double meanings, ambiguities, ellipses, truncated sentences, absurdly long and complicated sentences, through all this, or perhaps because of it, his story emerges with dazzling, moving clarity.

*My Big Apartment* is not a difficult novel to read, then, but it is a complex one, drawing on the multiplicity of every simple

act of language and every immediate emotion, offering pleasures both visceral and cerebral, sanguine and melancholic.
Before allowing the reader to discover those pleasures, I have
only to thank those without whom this translation would not
have been possible: Brian Evenson and Steven Rendall, for
their helpful suggestions and careful readings of various
manuscript drafts; Eleanor Hardin, for her sympathetic and
sensitive guidance from start to finish; and Christian Oster, for
his encouragement, good humor, and patient responses to my
many questions and for giving me the joy of reading and trans-
lating this wonderful book.

JORDAN STUMP

My name is Gavarine, and there's something I'd like to say.

Coming home one evening, I stopped at my door. Not my own door, actually. It was a glazed door, and beyond it lay only my building's front hall.

I had five pockets at my disposal that day, not one more, whose contents I needn't catalogue here. I searched through them, inflating some, deflating others, creating an ugly lump in this one, causing that one to protrude, convex, perpendicular to my thigh. Nothing. Everything, if you prefer, except keys.

This was all quite normal. I rarely put my keys in a pocket. I kept them in my briefcase. But somehow I'd lost my briefcase. And I'd never lost my briefcase before. That was what stopped me at my door.

For while I was distressed at the loss of my keys, I was dismayed, deeply dismayed, in fact, to find that the loss had occurred inside my briefcase. Or more precisely, with my briefcase. Because I was very fond of my briefcase. I wasn't all that fond of my keys, of course. I needed them, as everyone does, but I wasn't fond of them, no, I felt no love for them, unornamented as they were, moreover, by any sort of decorative key chain, for which I might perhaps have felt some attachment. On the other hand, yes, I was fond of my briefcase. I needed it, what's more. Imperiously so, in fact.

Let me be clear about this. Without my briefcase, I was nothing. I felt naked. I couldn't leave home without it. For instance, even just going out for bread, nothing more than bread, it was inevitably with me. I slipped the loaf inside, diagonally, the rounded heel protruding prowlike between the forward edge and the short leather strap that held the latch on that particular model.

For I owned a briefcase with a latch. That was my choice the day I bought it, and I wouldn't have wanted another. I soon grew accustomed to that latch, and now I could no longer imagine a briefcase, in a general sense, without such a latch. I'd made that briefcase my own. For want of a more complete definition of me, it would in fact be no exaggeration to say that, conversely, my briefcase had made me its own. Or, to cut this short, that in my own eyes, I was wholly contained within my briefcase.

And maybe, I sometimes told myself, that's why it's empty. Because it's true; there is nothing, apart from my keys, in my briefcase. So that, probably, I supposed, I might view myself as wholly held within it, in the company of my keys. In short, this – this way I, Gavarine, had of inhabiting my briefcase – was the opposite of an attempt to stand out from the crowd. As God is my witness, I never set out to be seen with my briefcase. On the contrary, seen was just what I set out not to be, and the idea that the gaze of my fellows might fall upon my briefcase and not upon myself was a reassuring one; it kept me from falling. Because, and this is another aspect of the thing, I was afraid of falling. I was expecting a fall. I was falling already, in fact. Expecting the worst, something worse than a fall, and falling all the while, that was more or less my idea of life.

2

When I realized that what I'd lost was my briefcase, with my keys inside, I concluded that my most basic right, given the circumstances, was to hesitate. I was aware of my rights. Nevertheless, I didn't intend to hesitate for long. I felt naked, of course, without my briefcase; I even wondered how I could have made it this far without it, and I didn't intend to let myself be caught standing here in this entryway. I hesitated briefly, therefore, between the two obvious solutions: either leave the building, in search of my briefcase and my keys, or else have the glazed door opened for me by pressing the intercom button.

Now it was no easy thing, leaving the building in search of my briefcase. As is often the case, I wasn't quite sure where I'd left it. I could certainly ponder that question outside, in some quiet spot, not too heavily traveled, without my briefcase, assuming, that is, that Anne Lebedel didn't open the door for me when I pressed the intercom button. And that I would know for sure once I had pressed the button.

I pressed it. Anne Lebedel didn't answer. Even though she lived in my apartment. She loved me. Or at least I, Gavarine, loved her. That's why she lived in my apartment. Because I loved her. Maybe also because she loved me. Or because I had a nice apartment. A big apartment, anyway. Maybe Anne Lebedel loved my big apartment. I'd done everything in my power to ensure that. I'd tried to make my big apartment a pleasant place. I'd decorated it myself, before Anne Lebedel came along. In preparation for her arrival. Even before I met her, I was already waiting for Anne Lebedel.

Her arrival followed soon after our first meeting. It all hap-

3

pened rather fast, I suppose. But that was hardly my fault. I never pressured Anne Lebedel. She'd moved in two weeks before.

Ruling out the possibility that she'd gone deaf, then waiting a bit on the chance that she was momentarily out of earshot or was on her way down to open the door, then pressing the button again, in vain, I concluded that she was out. I saw nothing unthinkable in that. In which case, either Anne would come home or she wouldn't. Would never come home again. Never. I found nothing extraordinary in that. It was in fact the opposite that would have surprised me: that Anne would come back, that she would come home again, that she would prolong my dream of keeping her there.

One way or another, I felt, faced with this new alternative – Anne coming back or not coming back – that it was best to go and think outside the building. I left, as discreetly as I could.

Outside, everything was much as it had been five minutes before, noisy, brightly colored, scarcely breathable. Mine was a bustling neighborhood, not far from asphyxiation. Nonetheless, trees grew in the square where someone handed me a piece of paper. The gist of the message was Stop the Massacre. It was a petition. I demurred. Apart from the fact that I'd been seen without my briefcase, I wasn't convinced that a stroke of the pen could put a stop to a massacre, especially not at this distance. And I was none too convinced of the petitioner's sincerity. I explained that for the dead, off in Africa, it was too late anyway and that, for the task of tending the wounded, feeding the children, and shooing away the flies, I would sooner work through some sort of accredited agency and send money. As soon as I had some money, that is. And even then, I wasn't sure I wouldn't send it to my sister instead. My sister was unemployed – and so was I, as it happened, but I made no mention of myself – and lived with her son in a dank ministudio. She had no telephone, never went to the hairdresser's. Obviously, there's no comparing. But she was my sister.

Now, had the man handed me a tract, rather than a petition, and had I had my briefcase, I would politely have tucked it away inside.

I was planning to avail myself, about an hour hence, after calling home about a half hour hence to see if Anne might be back, of the possibility of accessing my answering machine from afar, in case she still hadn't come back, to see if she might have left a message. Which I did, after venturing far from my neighborhood in search of my briefcase.

I ended up near my workplace, or former workplace, because I'd lost my job, before my briefcase, in the heart of the city, a few days before. Still, losing my job upset me less than losing my briefcase. I felt no attachment to my job. I felt an attachment to the money from my job, of course, which allowed me to pay my rent. But my briefcase was of no particular use to me in my job. I took it to work, of course, as I did everywhere I went. I set it down beside my desk. I had a desk job; I was almost an executive, in fact. On the threshold of an executive position, I'd hesitated, rather as I did at my door. That was what cost me my job. I didn't like telling people what to do and then verifying their compliance. It made me timid. I didn't like being timid. I wasn't naturally timid. Left to my own devices, I was never timid.

Anne didn't answer the phone and had nothing to say on the answering machine. She hadn't come home. I'd called from a phone booth near a small park. With no great optimism, of course, I then made for the bench in the park where I'd sat for a while with my briefcase in the late afternoon. I'd spent the day wandering through the city, and when it came time to be on my way home, when Anne, in theory, would be on her way home as well, I'd sat down on that bench and lingered. A foreboding kept me there. The idea – immediately banished from my mind – that Anne might not be home when I got there. That she would not be coming home. That this would be the end of our love. If that's the word. No one had ever spoken of love within those four walls over the previous two weeks, myself excluded. Anne was pure silence, silence made flesh. Scarcely even a presence. A shadow. Anne drifted through my big apartment, passed from one room to the next. Tried to settle in, unsettled, never finished unpacking. Never really started. Still trying to find her place, as if my place offered her none. I sat in the living

6

room, near the right-hand corner of the sofa, never moving as Anne endlessly drifted. Two weeks went by without Anne finding what she needed to make a place for herself in my apartment, and I began to foresee the day when she would ask if I minded her renting a little studio not too far away, for the sake of her independence. She would come and see me, of course. She would even have a place here, within the confines of my apartment, a place she might now finally find. A nook, some little corner, nothing more. It made me sick at heart to think that after two weeks it had come to this. But it hadn't come to this. Anne had simply left without a word.

This leaving without a word came as no real surprise. Hard to take, perhaps, but hardly surprising. Otherwise, after all, Anne Lebedel would have had to speak. And she didn't speak. Or spoke so little. She had only just begun to speak, with me, in my apartment. A few words, scarcely that. To tell me, generally, in a roundabout way, that my big apartment wasn't anything much. Not to her liking. So do something about it, I'd said. Why not do something about it? If, I said to her, there are alterations to be undertaken, why don't you point them out? Anne, I said. I called her Anne. She never called me anything at all. She didn't answer, changed the subject, smoothed back a stray lock of hair. I liked, as other men do, with other women, her little gesture as she tried to fix her hair, which never let itself be fixed. The strand fell back over her forehead. That way women have, never static, never definitive. That elusive beauty, their unawareness of that beauty. The best ones. The most beautiful. The most loved.

So Anne Lebedel didn't speak. Or spoke so little. Especially at the beginning. From the beginning, Anne said nothing. Not a word. None of those essential words that people say at the beginning. Nor any other, of course, lest in speaking she might approach one of the essential words, might evoke it in my mind. Anne Lebedel said nothing to bolster my confidence. Absolutely not. In case I might take it to heart. Anne intended to allow me no certainties. And so she said nothing, in the beginning, about that beginning. Although we hadn't really begun together. I'd had a head start. Of a few days. With each passing day, I loved Anne Lebedel more. And still nothing from her. No way to know. Hard to understand her drift.

8

Unless that was her way of fleeing me, in my big apartment. It's true; some evenings I scarcely saw her at all, except in bed, where she pretended to be sleeping. I pretended to believe it. She fell asleep. Not me.

Since our relationship had never really begun, it was no great surprise that it had now come to an end. Or, rather, that its end had come in the manner of its beginning. That's what it is, I told myself. So far, it hasn't begun. And what's happening now is that it isn't going to begin. It will never be. That's what's in store for you.

And yet I'd believed in it, in a sense. Just a little. Just enough to give Anne and her absence the benefit of the doubt. She was there, after all. So I could be forgiven for doubting her absence. But it was difficult. From a physical standpoint. Because of her physical presence. The more absent Anne's manner, the less I could forget she was there, physically. All that presence became unbearable. Sometimes I got up from the right-hand corner of the couch and went to meet her. I kissed her outright. Once, I'd made love to her. Completely forgetting that she still hadn't said anything. I cried out. Unequivocal words, right to her face. Wasted, I knew. Unequivocally. But that, at least, was one thing I wouldn't have to keep inside any longer. A deliverance, that's what it was, something I was giving up, before Anne's closed eyes, in exchange for nothing. Not that I felt delivered of much, really, in the end.

None of which kept me from talking. Coming home in the evening, with my briefcase, if Anne was there, I asked her what sort of day she'd had. Anne worked as a salesgirl for a big florist. In a tiny shop. One day I'd entered that little shop to buy some flowers. Intending to give them to Anne, whom I'd seen through the shop window. A ridiculous idea, of course, which furthermore never came to fruition. Anne disappeared into the back just as I crossed the threshold. I ended up face to face with the big florist, asking him for six pink roses. Not red, no. I know when enough is enough. I tried to slow down the process as the florist assembled the bouquet, so that Anne could come back into the shop. But it's not easy slowing down a florist. He alone had that power, as he assembled the bouquet, the power to slow me down.

But the big florist was brisk, his motions remarkably precise. No sooner had I taken out my change purse than there was my bouquet, standing upright in my left hand, leaving me only my right hand to open the change purse. I'd set my briefcase on the shelf affixed to the counter. I rooted through my change purse with two fingers, in search of the correct change, holding it open with a third. I extracted the coins in question, and at once the purse snapped shut. It had a spring closure. I'd bought it on the fly. I didn't dither that day. I'd lost my coin purse, a spring-less model, and needed another. So this was an emergency change purse, located on a display rack at the first opportunity, to hold the change in my pocket, loose in my pocket, jingling against the hand I kept in my pocket. This unmediated contact with my money grated on my nerves, because I always walked with one hand in my pocket and the briefcase in the other. I'd transferred the change from my pocket to the change purse, minus, of course, the price of the change purse. Anyway, standing at the counter before the big florist, I had some difficulty finding the proper change in that change purse. And the result of this was that, against all expectations, I succeeded in slowing down the process after all, leaving the florist standing idle and giving Anne a chance to reenter the shop.

I didn't offer her the bouquet, of course. It was a ridiculous idea, and I dropped it, dropping the flowers into a large green trashcan outside.

That was how Anne and I first saw each other.

Only later, at closing time, did we actually meet. I approached her. I'd told myself I really had no choice. I'm taking the liberty of speaking to you, I said, catching up with her on the sidewalk, because I have no choice. I tried to give you some flowers, three days ago, but I couldn't, it was impossible, your boss was there. And I wouldn't have had the courage anyway. But now it's absolutely vital that I know what you think of me. If you could give me some idea of that, not here, somewhere else, a café for instance, I could buy you a drink, it would only take a few minutes, and afterward, you understand, my mind would be at ease, I'd leave you alone.

You're planning to leave me alone? Anne had said.

If need be, yes, I'd said.

Well then, you can start now, Anne had said.

Right, I'd said.

We didn't get together right away. I had to go see the big florist again, and buy flowers from him, and see Anne, who knew about the flowers now, just what those flowers were intended for, and not give her the flowers. But after that, I couldn't go and wait for her at closing time anymore. I don't like to insist. Rather than waiting outside at closing time, I thought it better to buy flowers and not give them to her, but still, yes, to come back again for more. Surely I could buy flowers if I wanted to, after all. Surely Anne couldn't take offense at that.

Except that she did take offense, and surely she had every right. Although she said nothing because of her boss. It was all in her eyes, and for some time we exchanged glances, she and I, Gavarine, and rather severe those glances were. And then, one day, in Anne's eyes, there was a gleam. The sort of gleam that sometimes precedes a smile, among men, except that in this case it was a woman, and among women that prelude to a smile is like a breach, an opening, and I threw myself into it, and back I came at closing time. All right, five minutes, then, Anne had said, I'm meeting someone.

I spoke at some length that night, easily an hour, in fact, before Anne left, and Anne listened, even answered my questions but posed none of her own. Anne's first step, by way of saying nothing, or as little as possible, was to pose no questions. And this continued in the apartment, and I kept right on talking. And when I came home, with my briefcase, if Anne was there, settling in, or trying to, I would ask her about her day, with her big boss. But she never asked about mine. She didn't care what kind of boss I, Gavarine, had, if he was big or tough, if I sometimes ran into him in the course of my day. Nor did she care about what I did, at my desk, and I didn't care about what I did, at my desk, and I didn't care that she didn't care; yes, but the problem was the briefcase. I was amazed that Anne showed no curiosity about my briefcase. It's perfectly normal for a man to come home in the evening and leave in the morning with a briefcase, but less so, I thought, for the gaze of his companion never to land on his briefcase, as if that briefcase didn't exist. And while it is true that briefcases do exist, I said to myself, would it not be more accurate to say of mine that it occupies a place, at the very least, slightly superior to mere existence, that it is in fact alive? And, of course that's not what I ask of Anne, to realize that my briefcase, evidently, exists more profoundly than any other. No, what I ask of her is to see that it exists, plain and simple, like any other briefcase. And in fact, I'm not really asking for that either. I simply desire it, merely, secretly. But no. She doesn't see it.

At times I regretted that my briefcase stood upright when deposited on the floor near the couch. For as it happened, the leatherette was stiffened by a frame, which consequently al-

12

lowed the base to serve as a pedestal. Had I owned a soft-sided briefcase, made of cloth, for instance, and without a frame, such a briefcase, when empty, would inevitably have collapsed. In time, Anne would have found herself unable to contain her curiosity about such a briefcase, lying on its side, or sunk in upon itself, and so testifying to its own vacuity. In the end she would have had to ask me about it. And to ask a question concerning the emptiness in my briefcase would have been to come closer to me, Gavarine.

But I had ruled out the idea of exchanging my briefcase for another, one more apt to collapse, even if in so doing I might drag a question out of Anne. This, to me, was my briefcase, my kind of briefcase, indisputable, hard and fast.

Meanwhile, Anne displayed a sovereign disregard for my briefcase.

Less imaginable still, of course, was the thought that she might open it in my absence, in hopes of getting to know me better. Anne Lebedel didn't give a damn about me. I sometimes wondered what she was doing there, apart from poking vaguely at the roof I was offering to put over her head, to see if it really suited her. All the same, even devoid of any desire to know me better, she could have shown a little curiosity about that briefcase, as anyone else would. Because anyone, in Anne Lebedel's place, would eventually have opened that briefcase while I was out.

Anyone but Anne.

Except that I don't really know her, I told myself. Not at all. I've never foreseen her reactions or her desires, never once. Who knows, maybe she has opened it after all, my briefcase that is, and she's keeping it from me. Which would explain her silence, furthermore, it occurred to me. The emptiness, in my briefcase, yes, I told myself – not entirely convinced, though –

might well explain her silence. Even this one, this silence, I said to myself, the silence confronting me now. This present silence, concerning not the emptiness in my briefcase but her own absence, Anne's absence. My briefcase, not the emptiness in my briefcase but the absence of my briefcase, I told myself, might explain Anne's silence concerning her own absence, Anne's absence, if in my absence she had slipped a note concerning her own absence, Anne's own absence, into my briefcase. So that, I said to myself, that might be why, yes, why I must, having failed to find Anne, find my briefcase. Because she might have slipped a note into it this morning, before I left for work, for my workplace. A word of explanation. More precisely, a word of farewell. And that would be ideal. The most perfect failure.

And that was just what I was looking for at that point. Perfection. Wholeness. Because, yes, something was missing in my unhappiness that night, something to make it complete. A note, maybe just a single word.

You can't count on it, though, I told myself. Assuming the worst, or the best, depending on how you look at it, if I do end up finding that note, in my briefcase, with my briefcase, I'll get over it. I know myself. Disaster is nothing new to me. I know all about disaster. What I don't know, on the other hand, in my unhappiness, what I'd really like to experience, once and for all, is hell. But, I must admit, if hell is my goal, I still have a long way to go. Well, I said to myself. Maybe it's just a matter of quantity. Of accumulation. Deep down, hell might be nothing more than the sum of its parts. An overflow. Just a question of time, maybe.

There's one thing that bothers me, though, I said to myself. Which is that I don't really believe this business about a note. Aside from which, there's virtually no chance of finding my briefcase. On the other hand, one thing is certain. If Anne hasn't come home when I call again, in a while, I won't go home either. I'm not going back to an empty apartment, an apartment full of her absence. Even if I do find my keys, inside my briefcase.

So maybe I don't need to find my keys. Because even if I did, Anne probably wouldn't be there for me to say to her, for example, I found my keys, I'd lost them, all the things I'd need to tell her, because they happen to me in this life, this life with her, which would no longer be my life with her, then, because she wouldn't be there, and so there would be no need to tell her. But even if she were, I said to myself. She wouldn't listen. Here's what happened to me today, in this life of mine, now, with you, I lost my keys, and then I found them again, incredible, isn't it, I'd say, and she wouldn't be listening. No. It's just the briefcase that bothers me. What am I going to do about the briefcase?

I know, I said to myself.

Before the little park, this afternoon, I'd taken a break. The park wasn't a break; it was a halt. I'd sat down in that park to think. Not in the café. In the café, I'd sat down to ask the waiter for something. Something to drink, of course, there wasn't much else I could have asked him for. After which, drinking, unthirsty, I watched the waiter come and go. People came into the café, and I waited to watch them go out. When the next one goes out, I said to myself, I'll go out too. But when the next one went out, I, Gavarine, stayed behind. I waited for the next one. And so on. I couldn't bring myself to leave. I finally left when someone else came in. I needed some point of reference. And it was difficult. Not easy to go out when someone else is coming in, I'd said to myself. That sense of missing out on something, at the very least. That painful impression of a difference. That palpable divide, a definitive gulf forever separating you from the one coming in, as you go out.

I didn't think much about my briefcase in that café. On the contrary, it was there to free me from thinking. Besides, I was too busy watching the others. So I might have left my briefcase there, forgotten it. Or, if you prefer, forgotten myself. That happens to me sometimes. Much the same thing, in the end.

The surest way to find out about the briefcase was to go and talk to the waiter. I entered the café. But the waiter hadn't seen my briefcase. Had no memory of my briefcase. But you must, I reminded him, a briefcase with a latch, deep brown, a triangular flap for the latch. No, said the waiter. He shook his head. Stop shaking your head, I told him, I understand, it's all right.

I went outside. I wondered how the waiter could have failed to see my briefcase. I'd long since been convinced that only I, Gavarine, went unnoticed. Whereas my briefcase, on the other hand. Well. He's only a waiter, I told myself. I don't walk around with my briefcase for the sake of waiters. There are others, thankfully.

I called home again. Silence. Around me, within me, I must admit, night was falling. It was late. Late in my life as well. I waited for that sensation to grow clearer. It didn't grow clearer. Now I was waiting for unhappiness to stop knocking at my door. Waiting for it to take shape. An ulcer, maybe. Yes, I said. That might be the thing. Something physical, where thought would have no place. Into which thought would never enter.

No. I need thought, I said to myself. Or, rather, I don't need to be deprived of thought. What I need is something else. Suddenly, there it was. I need to be flat on my face. For the moment, here and now, I can carry on. There's nothing I can do, in fact, but carry on. Right, I said to myself. Let's carry on. And let's keep an eye out. Let's not lose hope.

Now, through the yellow streets, beneath the lights, I walked. No longer looking for my briefcase. Now I was looking for a hotel. My briefcase was ancient history. Forgotten. Erased from my life. I felt naked without it, to be sure. I couldn't get used to that. But I didn't miss my briefcase. No. What I missed was just a briefcase, any briefcase.

The next day I would buy another.

Even if Anne were to come home now, I would buy another.

I called Anne from a hotel, the first I came across. Far from home, on a dark street only faintly lit by the neon sign. Still not there. Never would be again. After I hung up, I said a few words to the clerk at the front desk. I would have said a few words to anyone, any words at all. No answer. He was sleeping in his chair. Come on, it's not the middle of the night, I said. You can't possibly be asleep, you could at least answer me. How'd you like this in your face? he said. He opened an eye, raised a fist. Why not? I said. The receptionist closed his eye again. Go to bed, he said, you have the key, the room number; leave me the hell alone. I was joking, I said.

The room was small, ugly, angled. I didn't brush my teeth, having no toothbrush. In any case, between my teeth, over which I did nevertheless run one finger, having first run it under the water, from the tap, which squeaked, no detritus lurked. Not surprising, since I'd had no dinner. I had eaten lunch, on the other hand, but nothing remained of it, nothing that my index finger could dig up. It pleased me to have skipped a meal. That's a start, I said to myself. A start to what? I said to myself. To hunger, I joked. Seriously, I could easily see myself as an

18

ascetic. But I wasn't hungry. And should I feel hungry in the morning, I harbored no illusions, I would eat. It would take more than this to make me skip two meals. More than the absence of a woman, even Anne Lebedel, whom I loved. Because I was perfectly capable of loving, of continuing to love Anne Lebedel, despite her absence, and of suffering, in my love for her, all the more grievously because she was absent. And I was perfectly capable of suffering, of continuing to suffer, of progressing in my suffering. And that first tear that then appeared, in the very corner of my eye – a bit prematurely, really, since after all Anne might simply have met with some delay as she was coming home, I told myself – did not rule out the possibility of other tears, heavier, more fully formed.

Because I could weep, I could even weep, nothing was alien to me that might allow an acceptance of pain, or an easier access to it. Pain was my bailiwick. Or, better, a lover. One I knew just how to handle. Whose coming never came as a surprise. Whose signs, whose ways I intimately understood. Who had no secrets from me. By leaving me, Anne was only bringing me closer to pain. I should be grateful. She'd given me back the pleasure of suffering. That old feeling, as if I were inside myself, uneasy, desperate to get out. That endless yearning, pacing circles inside my skull. That longing to cry out, always satisfied in the end. That warm pleasure I find, crying out.

I'm a lucky man, I told myself. Tonight I'll sleep in this miserable hotel, between two nightmares, which two I don't know, because my imagination strains, yes, it strains to imagine something worse, and tomorrow I'll call home. Anne will answer or not, is leaving me or has left me, or in any case will leave me, and I'll go and buy myself a briefcase.

And so, the next morning, I called. I found a message on the machine. I tried to sit down, but there was no chair next to

19

the telephone. It was a brief message, too brief. I had to play it again. It wasn't Anne. It was another woman. What other woman? I asked myself. She'd said her name, but her enunciation left something to be desired. It's been a long time, she said. I don't know if you remember me. Marthe, she said, or Maggy, or maybe George, although George. No. Here's my phone number, she said.

It was a Paris number. She must have been a very ancient woman, from a distant era of my life, and I struggled to recall the name she'd so garbled in her message. A struggle made no easier by my inability to remember any woman's name, or face. At best I might remember a smell, a patch of skin, a breast, yes, maybe, I said to myself. Just possibly, yes, maybe a breast, I can see one now, I said to myself, that's right, two, in fact, come to think of it, she was a girl with extraordinary breasts, it's coming back to me now, if ever I've known a really great pair of breasts in my life, those were the ones, tapered, full, with, to top it all off, that slight difference between the one nipple and the other, a difference that made all the difference, a lavish gift that no woman has offered me since, the gift of knowing that I could touch one breast and still not have taken the full measure of her bust, that on the contrary I would do well to consider the other one in all its singularity and not as a complement whose sense can only be grasped within the context of that always rather troubling duality, in which the eye, like the hand, but also like the mind, has some difficulty finding a firm purchase, caught up as they are, all three of them, in the perfect, circular congruence of the objects they ogle, paw, and conceptualize. With no possibility, mind you, of subjecting them to some sort of reduction or division, for on the contrary it is forever their synthesis that imposes itself, ineluctable, like a thing somehow fated to be.

20

Yes, I said to myself, it was long ago, that was, it was long ago that a woman one day gave me a gift of that sort. They soon stopped giving me gifts, never to be seen on my saint's day, my birthday, all so long ago. The worst thing, I said to myself, was that, knock on wood, I am, in a physical sense, relatively attractive, and powerfully built as well, and, but for my character, for what my character has become, over time, I might well be capable of being loved; but there we are, I'm not, loved that is, going about it the wrong way no doubt, too lovable probably, too loving, the old story, love is what those who love lack most, oh, I said to myself, now it's coming back to me. Marge. I'd forgotten Marge. That's who it was, who called me and wants me to call her back. How old is she now? My God, I said to myself, my age, of course, she's my age, how can that be, how could she have grown so old, I can't believe it. She must be married, children who could be my sons, a husband who could be my father, she was fond of older men back then, myself excluded, fortunately, I only seemed old, to her, when I was twenty-five, it was my seriousness that excited her, it put her in quite a state, that seriousness of mine, it made her laugh, and then. And then nothing. We lost touch, I don't know how.

And furthermore, I said to myself. Furthermore Marge did not have particularly lovely breasts. I've got them mixed up. The breasts must have been someone else. Whose name, yes, escapes me. But not Marge, no. Marge's breasts, it's coming back to me now, were nothing much, an absence at most, the strangeness of that sort of absence in a woman, the emotion it arouses, perhaps too ephemeral. I never loved Marge the way I should have. She was the one who. That shows how long ago it was. Back before I learned how to go about loving someone. The progress I've made in that area since.

Except that it isn't Marge I love, I reminded myself. I love

Anne, who hasn't come home, who's left no word for me. Who won't be coming home. She's gone off to someone else's place, that's what it is. In the meantime, she must be at the florist's. Let's go by, I said to myself. And see. I'll deal with the briefcase later.

I saw her. Behind the front window of the florist's shop. She wasn't a florist, really. If she were somewhere other than in that florist's she would have been a secretary. Or a salesgirl. Anne had no baggage. Not like me, I smiled. I was thinking of my briefcase. But especially of Anne, who had no baggage. I liked that. An uncomplicated girl. Not stupid, visibly, a girl with character and, above all, that physique. Not that she was beautiful. Anne wasn't beautiful, no. She had a certain charm. Perfectly innocent, at first, and then that look. When your eyes met hers. So rarely did your eyes meet hers that when they did you felt as though you'd captured her gaze. Caught it. Such at least was the feeling I had once. Of having seen and then held – only in my memory, nothing more than that – Anne's gaze. My love for her ran purely on memory. The way you keep a woman inside yourself, in spite of her absence. After that, I'd locked eyes with Anne too infrequently to presume that her gaze had settled on me. No more than Anne had settled into my apartment. But in any case, that gaze was on my mind. And I wasn't about to forget it.

I was already having to remember it as I took up my position on the sidewalk opposite the shop. This was a start. I couldn't see Anne's face, concealed behind five flowers. Roses again. It was the leaves, more than anything, that hid Anne from me. The customer shielded her as well, as if she had set out to erect every possible barrier between herself and me, every possible thing, object, being. That had never been hard for her.

Then, inevitably, the customer paid for his flowers and

emerged. Anne appeared to me behind her counter. She was picking up the leaves, the fallen leaves. She looked out the window, dreamily, I'm not sure that's the word, but in any case still not seeing me. The boss remained invisible, perhaps simply absent.

I had to cross the street. I had, moreover, if I wanted her to see me, to push open the door of the shop, so that the bell, set aquiver by the moving door, would tinkle. And even then, she didn't see me right away. And then she couldn't believe it was really me. I could see that. She too, in her own way, had always found it hard to believe in my presence.

It's me, I had to say, to help me believe it myself, in my presence. I felt so out of place in that shop. Like a place you once knew but have since left, and when you come back it's already different; others have already left their mark. It's me, I said, then, whereas clearly what I should have said was, It's you. So it's you. You, in this shop, vanished without a word, back in this shop as if nothing had happened.

I can see it's you, Anne said to me. I'm alone here this morning; I don't have a lot of time. I didn't want to disturb you last night.

I almost asked her why. Why she didn't want to disturb me. But I didn't. I know what she would have said, or wouldn't have said. She wouldn't have said: I didn't dare disturb you to say I was leaving you. She wouldn't have dared say that. And that's not what she was thinking anyway. But it's what she was about to tell me. And I didn't want to hear her say it. Leaving me meant nothing to Anne, I could see it in her eyes. And she wouldn't have wanted to disturb me, in the end, to tell me that she was leaving me and that it meant nothing to her. You only disturb people for serious matters. And leaving me wasn't a serious matter, to Anne. She must have been thinking I should

23

have known she would leave me. And she was right. I was willing to admit that. In the end, we were in complete agreement, agreeing that she would leave me, that I would suffer, and that she wouldn't trouble herself over such trifles. Agreeing that we would now say no more about it and that I would now be on my way. That I would walk out of the shop. Agreed.

Hey, she said, you don't have your briefcase.

This was all happening a little too fast for my tastes. I understand, of course, that it's natural to take an interest in people you're about to leave – it's perfectly normal, they no longer mean anything to you, you can ask questions, the answers cause no pain, no confusion – but this was all happening a bit fast, as I said, and with regard to the briefcase, I didn't have an answer ready for Anne. I had no answers for anything at all, and now I would have to come up with something. This, I must admit, put me in a bad mood. I was unhappy before, of course, rather exceptionally so, to be sure, I imagine that's clear, but not in a bad mood, no. Rather, I viewed the void opening up before me with the serenity that has always been granted me by the knowledge that I will inevitably fall into it, and caught up as I was in this acceptance of my lot, I had even begun, mentally, to leave the shop, thinking of Anne, of the mere memory of her that would be left to me, a cruel memory, then, when Anne, suddenly, the real, live – although that was something of an overstatement – Anne, here present – I know what I mean – held me back a moment longer with a question.

Now that the question had been posed, of course, I intended to answer it. I was already on my way out, and I wasn't about to just quietly drift away. But I had no intention of gratifying Anne; that shouldn't be too difficult to understand. By giving her the truth. I'm no moralist, but as I saw it, she didn't deserve the truth. Especially not mine.

24

I don't have a briefcase anymore, I said.

My tone was unambiguous. The only inference that Anne could draw was that I'd decided to stop going out with my briefcase. She asked no further questions.

We parted without another word, although in my gaze I sought to convey all the density of a situation that, although drawing to a close, was, it seemed to me, nonetheless worthy of some sort of echo. A kind of epilogue, in other words, to which I put an end by turning on my heel. Until you reach the door, I said to myself, you won't turn around. I reached the door. Now walk past the front window, I told myself. Five meters, it's not the ends of the earth. And at the third meter I turned around. But, let me make this quite clear, I did so deliberately. I'd changed my mind. No reason, I'd told myself at the third meter. No reason, just because she'd abandoned me like a dog, to deprive myself of the final torment of a final glance. And so I looked at her. And it hurt me. Particularly because, already, she wasn't looking at me.

I entered the first barbershop I found. I needed to clear my head. I'd been to the barber many times in my life, but never the same one twice. I don't like barbers' questions. Happily, the number of barbershops had exploded in the previous few years. People couldn't get enough haircuts. Getting my hair cut was my way of fitting in. Very short, I said.

I came out with a twinge of regret. At not having offered my neck to the razor. To finish me off, the barber had pulled out a razor, a real one, old-fashioned, the kind barbers hold open with two fingers, recalling at best a stylized swallow, at worst a bird of ill omen. I looked at it longingly, but I can't stand the sight of my own blood, and I soon abandoned the idea. But once I was outside, my regret passed just as quickly. Everything passes, I said to myself, thankfully.

That, I don't know why, was when I thought of my keys, the copy of my keys, still in Anne's possession. I hadn't thought to ask for them back. She must have left them in the apartment, I told myself. That would be logical. In any case, if she was thinking of leaving me, last night, when she left me, she would have left the keys in the apartment. Unless she'd kept them, unthinking. That would be more or less like her. But it scarcely mattered, in the end. I didn't need her keys. I didn't even need my own now. I really didn't feel like going home. I could, if necessary, go to a locksmith's, a locksmith's isn't home, it's a kind of antechamber, with respect to home, and that would give me some time to regain my desire to go home, while I explained the situation to the locksmith, and while I waited for him to find a moment to see to me, but no: he would probably doubt my credibility, I probably wouldn't look enough like someone who wanted to go home, he would want some sort of proof. He would ask for my papers. No thanks.

In any case, I said to myself, if nothing else, losing my keys at least stopped me going home, last night. If I had gone home, it would have taken me longer to reach the conclusion that Anne was leaving me. So that saved me some time, and I'm not unhappy about that. Unless she'd taken her things with her, which is of course the most likely scenario, and then I would have noticed right away. She would have left a few clothes, a few things, of course, once again unthinking. Just enough to make it clear that others were missing. All the more reason not to have gone home, I said to myself, then, all the more reason not to go home, and to start trying to forget her. Which won't be easy, I know, and so, for that very reason, I might as well get to it. And, while I'm waiting to forget her, I'm going to buy that briefcase. That, at least, will be that.

And so, without so much as a glance in the window, I entered the first luggage shop I came across. I wasn't going to be choosy about the model. In short, I'd turned a page, and with my hair now cropped, I felt painfully new. This was no time for dithering. That's fine, I said, when the salesgirl showed me her six varieties, whichever you like best will do nicely.

Nevertheless, I insisted on emptying the one she handed me – the most expensive, but I couldn't blame her – of its ball of crumpled newsprint in order to test its rigidity. It was a heavy briefcase, I found, with a solid frame, and, even empty, dangling from my arm, gave an impression of not being so. Better suited to my needs, in a sense. I left with the briefcase hanging heavily from my hand and told myself that the time had now come to call Marge.

I'd like to avoid a possible misunderstanding here: I was

27

thinking of Anne. It was because I was thinking of Anne that I decided to call Marge. The one did not drive out the other. The one, on the contrary, led to the other. Led to the other logically, like a road stretching out before me, on which, injured myself in a series of successive collisions with women, I'd left a number of corpses behind me. For even if she lived on inside me as a wound, Anne was nonetheless dead, buried under tons of lucidity, lost forever to the sort of man I was, a man fully conscious of the immutability of things. She would never come back; she was far away now, frozen in failure's enduring statuary, or, if you prefer, a figurine spinning in the maelstrom of disaster, but, in any event, with the present and future fading fast, there was nothing for it but to let the past swallow her whole, and the only thing to do now, which was quite a lot actually, was move in the opposite direction. Hello, I thus said in a telephone booth, again the first one I came across, with no one but myself there to see me or, consequently, to judge me. It's Luc.

Amazingly, I wasn't speaking to an answering machine. Nor the sister, the husband, the lover, the cleaning lady. No, that was Marge on the other end of the line, Marge's voice, different of course, hoarse, a little worn, but it really was Marge, incredibly, and I couldn't help but wonder at this turn of events. This was not how things usually happened in my life, that, having left me a message asking me to call her, a woman who had disappeared from my existence ten years before was now waiting on the other end of the line, ready to respond, as if Heaven, not content with bringing about this miracle, had now, in its infinite mansuetude, stamped it with its own imprimatur. I might have thought I was dreaming, but that's not really my style. I never dream. I record. I acknowledge. After which I add or subtract. That's my life.

28

Well, said Marge, and I listened to her voice, not quite believing it but believing it all the same, since it was, after all, her, a woman from the past, back in the picture, sketchily drawn, badly lit, the sound quality only so-so, certainly not very faithful, so anyway, she was saying to me, I was watching television last night. It was a TV movie, with an actor, I can't remember his name, you see him sometimes, he looked like you, and that made me want to call you.

I took a deep breath. I'm not that fond of comparisons, but I asked Marge if he was at least a handsome actor. Very attractive, said Marge, very attractive, I'm sure you know him, always minor roles, police chiefs or ministers, always with short hair, yes, she affirmed as I was about to pose another question, he's good looking, obviously, I wouldn't have called you if he weren't, would I?

There, despite that somber voice, distant, conferring on her utterances an import they didn't have, like lightweight prose in ponderous translation, there I recognized Marge. Her rather personal logic. Her directness as well, I remembered that now, which used to shock me, way back when. No danger of that today. Nothing shocked me anymore. It's true, I said to myself, nothing shocks me. Although everything wounds me. That's how it is. What have you been up to? I said to her, hoping to bring about a shift in the conversation, whose focal point, in the long term, I preferred not to occupy. Do you have children?

Two, she said, and I observed a moment of silence. And a husband, she added. Jealous. It's complicated. Can we meet?

Meet? I said.

Yes, she said. See each other.

That must be possible, I said.

Are you married?

Hmm? What did you say? It's a bad connection.

Married, she repeated.

Oh, I said. No, not particularly.

What do you mean, not particularly?

I'm not married, I said. I'm not married at all.

Can we meet in two hours?

In two hours? I exclaimed. You mean today?

Yes, I mean today. In two hours.

It depends where, I said.

At the pool.

I was getting caught up. In what I didn't know, but I was getting caught up.

It depends which pool, I said.

She gave me the name.

It's in the ninth arrondissement, she said.

I was in the ninth.

What address? I said.

She told me.

I've got it, I said. But I don't have a swimsuit.

You'll also need a bathing cap, Marge said to me. It's mandatory. You can rent everything you need at the front desk. See you soon. Kiss kiss.

Kiss kiss. That's not what I said in response; it's what I said to myself, repeated it, said it again. Kiss kiss, that's what she'd said. Emotion flooded over me. A woman who, returning to me after ten years, says kiss kiss. Just like that, as if there were still something going on, something with me, something that had never ended. Kiss kiss. That's what Anne used to say too, on the phone, the first few days. And this was the same. The same emotion.

I drew no conclusions. In all my life, I'd never known a trustworthy conclusion. Things happen, one after another, that's all. I merely pondered where I might find a swimsuit. I had no intention of renting a suit at the front desk. This was a meeting, not a surrender.

So at least I told myself.

And soon I was in a vast sporting goods store at the Forum des Halles. It was the closest one, and I didn't have much time to spare. I located the swimming aisle, hesitated between boxer- and brief-style suits, finally chose a pair of black briefs, bought some goggles, seduced by their elegant lines, acquired a white bathing cap, let's see now, I said to myself, am I forgetting anything? Of course, I said, how stupid of me, a towel. A bath towel. There were none to be found. The swimming aisle was no place for drying off. I had no choice but to proceed to a housewares shop, in the vicinity of Châtelet, and buy a bath towel, bedspread sized and heavy and hence difficult to accommodate, for whose transport I was thus forced to purchase a gym bag on the sidewalk of the Rue de Rivoli, in front of the Samaritaine department store. All this had consumed an hour, and I still had more than enough time to arrive early. I dawdled in the metro, got off one train and on the next, with my towel and my bathing briefs in my bag and everything else in my briefcase, which I did not, however, decide to rechristen my satchel, too schoolchildish, or my attaché case, too long, it's a briefcase, it's my new briefcase, and I'm not going to let a silly swimsuit, also new, overturn my longstanding lexical habits.

I reached the pool fifteen minutes early, a municipal pool, emblazoned with the city logo. I was coolly received, not a word more than necessary, despite having never come to this place before, to this pool, and I was thinking that seeing as this was my first time, but after all I was used to such things, people are never particularly friendly with me, and of course the woman at the front desk could scarcely be expected to know why I was there, how exceptional all this was for me, coming to this pool, to see a ten-year-old woman, I know what I mean, but I bore her no ill will, the woman at the desk I mean, and even when she confirmed that the bathing cap was indeed mandatory, I cast her no indignant glances, but took the ticket she handed me and headed toward the locker room.

On the way I found three portholes offering an unobstructed view of the water, albeit at waist level. I bent double, and through one I glimpsed a small crowd, half naked, dribbling wetly in a universe of blue tile. Well, I told myself, it's a pool, you don't have to make a big deal of it. Pools are tiled.

I didn't see Marge. But I was early. And I might possibly have failed to recognize her. In her bathing cap. And then, she might have changed. Must have, in fact. In any case, I said to myself, it's too early for doubts. Go get yourself dressed, first.

At the door to the locker room, a man in blue took my ticket and tore it in half. I've never particularly liked having my tickets torn in half, same thing at the movies, I find it humiliating, as a situation, but, well, he was only doing his job, and I even asked him, amiably, how to proceed in the locker room. You'll need two francs, he said. It works on two-franc coins. I went through my pockets, found no two-franc coins, was told to go back to the front desk, went back to the front desk. I don't have any change, the woman at the cash register told me. You're joking, I said. Nothing I can do, said the woman. So what do I do? I said. You try to find two francs, she said to me. And how do I do that? I said. Wait for the next customer, the woman said to me. But I can't! I said. What do you mean, she said, you can't? Well, yes, I said, I can, of course I can. But it's not very convenient.

So I stood and waited at the front desk. Not directly in front of it, of course, I didn't want to be in the way. My greatest fear was that the next customer would be Marge, and I couldn't picture myself, after we'd embraced, I supposed, asking her for two francs. And most of all, we hadn't arranged to meet by the front desk. Although, I said to myself, she would see me fully dressed, and that would be better, wouldn't it, for a new beginning? But the next customer wasn't Marge. It was a man, fortunately, with no lack of change. He had two two-franc coins and agreed to grant me one. I returned to the locker room, asked the assistant how it worked, with the coin. In the slot, like that, he said to me, and then you close it and enter your code. Thanks, I said, and first I headed toward a changing booth in which I found one of those unhandy valet stands, made of red plastic, whose basin-like pedestal can scarcely accommodate a single shoe and over whose hanger, given the excessively narrow gap delimited by the rod, a pair of pants cannot be hung undeformed. In the booth, similarly cramped, I undressed straddling a puddle, sometimes leaning against the damp grainy wall, whose color, an ocher with fecal overtones, brought to mind memories of childhood, immediately dismissed. Soon I was in my swimsuit, a bit tight, I thought, whose cut, too daring for my tastes, would no doubt have been shown to better advantage by more tangible abdominals and, in a broader sense, a healthier diet. To be sure, I still enjoyed a view of my feet, but never would I extend a plumb line from above in the confidence that it would not graze my flesh, and this slight flaw in my verticality left me feeling more naked than I was, a sensation that, in my isolated existence, I'd lost the habit of experiencing in public.

Nevertheless, I emerged from the booth wearing my bathing cap, reluctant to pull it down over my ears, leaving it, I realized, ballooning atop my skull, carrying the valet stand slung with my gym bag in one hand and my briefcase in the other, and I stuffed it all, as best I could, into the snug slot of the cubbyhole assigned to me. For the code, I tapped out my date of birth, with little difficulty, for my date of birth did not remind me of

33

my birth, and that at least was a blessing. Besides, my birth has never been anything more to me than a string of numbers, one of those strings of numbers inscribed on your papers and in that area of the brain where affectivity has no place, dedicated solely to PIN numbers and salient dates from the annals of world history. I descended the steps toward the men's showers, positioned myself under a free head, and, with many a contortion, obtained a partial dampening from its hesitant diagonal drizzle of lukewarm water. After which, as one makes an entrance on stage, I traversed the footbath at a lively clip and headed straight toward the ladder at the deep end of the pool, into which I unhesitatingly immersed myself, completing the metamorphosis and becoming a swimmer. For a swimmer, I told myself, is the least visible element of a swimming pool's décor, and I was hoping not to be seen immediately. On the other hand, I was hoping to see, and soon, raising my capped and goggled Martian head above the water, I glanced around me, determined, from among the women striding through the footbath in rigorously unpredictable cycles, to identify the one I was awaiting.

A number of women appeared over the following fifteen minutes, from among whom I immediately excluded all who were not alone. For in light of our phone conversation, I told myself, Marge was scarcely likely to afflict me with the presence of a man, at her side after his stroll through the footbath, roughly synchronous with hers but from the opposite entrance, or of a woman other than the one I had chosen to await. As for the rest, the women alone, they bore her no resemblance, neither close nor distant. And so, swimming halfheartedly, vaguely wriggling my arms so as not to sink, sometimes wreathed in little eddies bearing witness to a spike in the curve of my exertion, then lying low for a time, swimming seriously toward the entrance-exit and the shallow end – distinguished from the other by a simple change of gradient in the pool's depths, emblematic of a purely transitional conception of difference – and so, with my face ever turned toward the footbath, I began to think to myself that Marge would not be coming. And of course this didn't upset me, habituated as I was to disillusionment, but it was unsettling all the same, for, lacking any certain knowledge that she would indeed not be coming, I couldn't wholeheartedly embrace the idea, in addition to which, from time to time, I was beginning to wish that she'd just left me alone.

And the result of this was that, at such moments, anticipating, in order to let the idea of her absence take root, that Marge would not appear, I would have been all the more unlikely to identify her from among the women walking through the footbath, surveying them as I was with an eye jaundiced in spite of myself by an intensifying exclusionary reflex. Soon I was excluding every woman a priori, all the while watching for the appearance of the one I remembered, spurred on more by reason than conviction.

But, setting these complications aside, I can affirm today, in all simplicity, that Marge did not then appear, and I concluded, for the moment, for lack of anything better, that she was late. And since my credibility as a user of the pool was ever more at risk of evaporating with every passing moment – my frothy stasis in the middle of the deep end having degenerated into an uneasy occupation of the shallow, amid the squeals and horse-play of the younger set – I now made the decision to swim, as everyone else was, the full length of the pool. Unhappily, I was facing the wrong direction, meaning that I would have to forego my view of the footbath as I made my way across the water. For that reason, I resolved to proceed through the deep end with all possible speed; then, on reaching the opposite side, I would cling to the edge and resume my watch.

So I cast off, immediately adopting a powerful propulsive movement known as the breast stroke, by means of which, in close proximity to a pool regular, my skull rhythmically broke the surface of the limpid water, tinted blue by its bed, my motions long and vigorous, my intakes and outflows of breath timed to the split second, and I reached the other side virtually amid the spume of my chance partner, who then abruptly reversed course with an ebullient thrust of the thighs. For my part, one hand clinging to the edge, I paused to let my heart decelerate, and as I had done several times before, shifting my goggles from orbits to temples for a clearer view, I stretched the rubber strap that held the lenses in place, but now it gave way under the force of the tension.

I tried to replace the strap, which is to say reinsert it into its clasp, a sort of valve, to be precise, with no axis, holding fast by pressure alone, but, I soon discovered, the clasp was gone, and I scanned the surface of the water in search of the small pink plastic quadrangle without which my goggles could be of no further use. After a moment, however, I realized that the clasp was slowly sinking.

I dove, stretching out my right hand, but the clasp eluded me, and I watched as it came to rest on the bottom, reluctant to follow. For such was the pressure exerted on my temples by the water, so relentlessly did it sap my forces, particularly the capacity for judgment required to evaluate the risks involved in prolonging my plunge, that I could not determine my best course of action, and in the end I opted for the solution, purely instinctive, but also compliant with certain objective physical principles, of returning to the surface. I gasped, then puffed, once more clinging to the familiar concrete rim, and as I resumed my scrutiny of the footbath, my goggles partially submerged, the rubber strap floating atop the water in my limp grasp, my accidental swimming partner appeared at my side, his length now complete. You've lost your clasp, he said.

He'd pushed his own goggles up onto his forehead. I was surprised to find him addressing me, but considerably more so that he had interrupted his exertions to do so. Meanwhile, he had asked me a question, and there was no denying that I had indeed lost my clasp. I chose not to take that risk. Yes, I said, and – just as, with that sort of amicable redundancy to which one resorts in hopes of facilitating a nascent relationship, people often supplement their words with a gesture or a glance – I cast my eyes toward the bottom, where, duly refracted, the scarcely visible blob that was my little clasp lay wavering. Just then, a woman came and joined my partner, to whom, I gathered, she was in some way linked, and very congenially inquired into the cause of my partner's and my coming together.

We outlined the situation for her in broad strokes, relieving each other periodically as we set out our brief account, which by various means I, for my part, tried to render less dramatic, refusing, for example, to align my gaze with theirs as they stared into the depths as if a human life were at stake. But this was not enough to prevent the woman, clearly delighted at the opportunity, from diving and disappearing, and I had no choice but to wait, uncertain of the pose I should adopt, until she reappeared with my clasp, which alas I did not know how to put back into place.

Wait, said the man, you're not at the groove. And, leaving me no time to perceive that groove, concerning which I nevertheless expressed a certain curiosity, now that he had revealed its existence, he took the clasp from my hands, followed by the goggles, and I was beginning to wonder if, waiting for a woman in a pool like this, I offered such an appearance of distress to the world around me that my fellows were irresistibly compelled to come to my assistance, or if, long before this, everything about me, everything about my attitude and my conduct had been crying out for such solicitude. In any event, it irritated me, and I probably did not thank my couple as I should have. Besides, with all this to-do, I had relaxed my vigilant observation of the footbath, and I abandoned my benefactors, rather coolly, to head toward the shallow water, where I stayed for a moment, my torso unambiguously immersed, pivoting slowly, scrutinizing not only the footbath but also the whole of the pool, toying with the hypothesis that Marge had made her appearance somewhere in the course of this interlude. Failing to spot her, I then bolstered that hypothesis with the supposition that after all this time without her, I mightn't have recognized her, or that after all this time without me, she mightn't have recognized me. That was when I saw her.

She wasn't beautiful, it's true, but, I'm taking a risk here, a risk of not being believed, I, Gavarine, have never liked beautiful women. By beautiful I mean – where women are concerned, that is – those whose every secondary characteristic, by virtue of that beauty, disappears into their most distant reaches, most often irretrievably, so that when you scratch at that beauty you only skin yourself, uncovering nothing that, set alongside that beauty, might serve to bring it out.

I could put this differently by saying that I, Gavarine, am blinded by beauty, that beauty obstructs my view, most particularly my view of that beauty itself, a contradiction only in appearance – precisely – expressing, it seems to me, the harsh truth of a concept that in its search to incarnate itself succeeds only in occulting its object.

So anyway, she wasn't beautiful, fortunately. She didn't have a beautiful face. On the other hand, there was in her face an infinity of readily discernable undertones; thus, in the excessive proximity of her two eyes, there was an echo of a tension, similarly around the narrow mouth a sort of density to the skin, on which the lips, digging into it, the skin I mean, in order to blaze a trail toward expression, had inflicted some tribulation, some originary trauma, in response to which the entire face had chosen to harden or rather, in compensation, to plump.

For it's true, she had full cheeks, and in a general sense it seemed as though her sensory organs, the nose included, and a delicate nose it was, had resolved to take up as little space as possible, yes, but a central and definitive space, which her

39

cheeks, forehead, and chin had struggled in vain to wrest from their control, a utopian ambition they did not intend to encourage but rather, on the contrary, serenely repressed through a full and resolute occupation of their site.

Serenely, I say, for there was something serene about her forehead and chin, and her cheeks as well, rounded despite the hardness that seemed to encase them, producing the paradoxical effect of a softness, but this serenity was intermingled with a force, the force of her mouth and eyes, now aimed in my direction.

As is my custom, of course, I didn't quite believe it, but I couldn't see anyone else she could be staring at as she was – and with such dazzling tenderness, what's more – someone standing five yards before her, amid a widely-scattered group, from which I emerged distinctly, surrounded as I was by physiognomies too immature, I believed, to have attracted such insistent attention.

The furtive smile on her thin lips – for her mouth was not only narrow – afterward seemed a mere mirage, but, placing my trust in my short-term memory, I concluded that it had indeed existed, however fleetingly, and I was searching for some confirmation that it had indeed been directed toward me when, with her gaze alone, this time, she skewered me for a quarter of a second.

It was one of those quarters of a second that count in a man's life, the sort you can count on the fingers of one hand, while so many others pass by, stillborn, indistinguishable from their fellows, scarcely successive, caught up in the impression of totality that sweeps off all the ordinary days – virtually the lot of them, to tell the truth. So I'm not quite sure how I greeted this second glance, surely not with a hint of a smile, probably gravely, but with what sort of gravity I didn't know, or how she interpreted it, as indifference, or trepidation, or some sort of perverse coldness. The best thing for me to do now, I said to myself, for I'd made my decision, and I could find no reason to unmake it, is probably to go to her, say something to her, some word that might compensate for my look, or serve as a caption for it, but what word, I said to myself, what word would be neither too strong nor too weak? I'm not going to talk to her about the weather. Which is an idiotic topic anyway, in an indoor pool, a sure sign of imbecility or even madness. Well, I told myself, just stop thinking about it. Just go to her, get close to her, get moving, and soon it'll be too late to back out, you'll see, I encouraged myself, warmly but with a tinge of anticipatory reproach, as I wasn't sure how I would react to this suggestion.

But once I reached her, everything seemed simple. She was staring at me, and I didn't know quite what to do with such a form of address, respond to it tit for tat, grasp the opportunity for some opening gambit – what about, I briefly thought, saying hello to her? but I abandoned that solution, the lazy way out, it seemed to me – so what do I say, I said to myself, well, say what you feel, of course, you big dope, the obvious truth of what you feel, how you're drawn to her, irresistibly drawn, some short little sentence, anything will do.

But, I now realize – a bit late, I admit, but the error is not irreparable – it is rather to the reader that I really should address two or three words at this point. A little clarification might be in order, yes, although he, the reader, has probably already understood that when I speak of this woman, the woman I'd just glimpsed in the pool, I'm not speaking of Marge, no. Because she wasn't Marge. And from my first glimpse of this woman, this woman I'd immediately told myself was her, not Marge, but her, I'd simply stopped thinking about Marge, that should be clear by now. So it was this new woman I had come here to meet and not Marge, who would certainly have changed a great deal more than this. In any case, given the date, Marge could only have been less young.

So this was the woman I now approached, no longer waiting for Marge, no longer wondering whether Marge would appear, or not appear, or had already appeared, moot questions all. I only had eyes for this woman, who seemed to be waiting for me, genuinely, as I'd waited for her, as I'd waited for every woman, yes, including Anne Lebedel, in my big apartment, and now I need to add another word, a word about that apartment, because now everything is happening very fast, it was all happening very fast, so let's start a new paragraph, things will be clearer.

That woman, then. The woman standing in the shallow water, whom I'd approached with my cap ballooning atop my head and nothing to say to her that didn't seem sadly inadequate in the face of her eloquent silence. That woman, who was not Marge, near whom I now stood, almost close enough to touch. Well, that woman, I'd noticed this, of course, from the beginning, that woman had a very large stomach.

Now, I should say that I feel no particular attraction to pregnant persons. On the contrary. I see them as sympathizing with the other side. The men's side, the men who made them pregnant. And I feel no fondness for men who make women pregnant, nor for the women, consequently, who let them. I've always thought it slightly wanton, the way they offer themselves up to the other, the way they bear the fruit of their error as if it were the most natural thing in the world, or proudly, I don't know, as if I didn't exist as well, as if my exclusion from the whole affair were not enough, as if on top of that I had to keep out of their way, and hold my breath, and in fact such women could scarcely care less whether I exist or not, whether I'm breathing normally or not; they simply pass by, superior, haughty – one of them even jostled me once. So I feel no particular attraction to them, but now, suddenly, none of that mattered. This woman, with her very large stomach, had now rejoined my side. Her smile made that crystal clear, and I clung to it like a life preserver – I know, this was happening in a pool, too bad, I'm sticking with the life preserver image, and for a very good reason: in that gaze, a little above her smile, I did not drown. No, my life was saved. While you're staring at her, nothing too terrible can happen, I told myself. It's only when you open your mouth that it can all suddenly go wrong, particularly given the notion now entering your mind, the idea that when dealing with a woman of this sort, it is customary to inquire into the age of her condition, the date of its origin, you'd best drop that thought right now, if you ask me, you don't know her well enough.

And, after all, I said to myself, since you don't know her well enough, you needn't be in any hurry to speak to her, to let slip who knows what words, and maybe upset this whole scene, and her as well, who knows, or at the very least wipe that wonderful expectant look off her face and force her to make some sort of response, drawing her out of herself, from within whom she is for the moment hailing me with such benevolence, not knowing who she's dealing with, it's true, which probably isn't such a bad thing. The ideal strategy, then, would be to prolong the moment, because a moment is all it is, inevitably, I can see that, in three seconds everything will have changed, I will have taken the floor, I will have taken her with my words, simply because she's smiling at me, on the pretext of a smile, I will have forced myself upon her with my words, and here I am cynically seeking the appropriate opening, knowing full well that I'll say nothing new, childlike, unmitigatedly sincere. Whereas a smile.

Excuse me?

Yes, a smile. Smile back at her.

How do I do that?

Well, you might cast off some ballast from your gaze, old man, to begin with; try to make it a little less insistent, not so heavy, not so tense. You know each other now, after all, if only slightly. A glancing gaze, if you like. Soon gone, soon forgotten. Out of the way. Like a caress, if you prefer.

Really?

Yes indeed, my dear boy, and you might do something with your lips while you're at it. Don't make a sound. You don't have to grin, that's not what I said. Just unclench them a little. I mean unclench your jaws a little. If you could only see how clenched those jaws of yours are just now.

So, in sum, relax. Just forget for a moment that this woman has already begun to mean something to you, to mean quite a

44

lot, in fact, forget that the mere sight of her has stripped you of your faculties, stop thinking about your faculties, just try to seem nice, cordial, in a word, relaxed. Try to think of something else, in other words. Well no, that's not exactly what I mean, the opposite, in fact, but try to inject a little serenity into your thoughts, would you? Look, I really don't care anyway, I said to myself, figure it out for yourself. This is your problem, after all.

And I did more or less as I was told. About the lips, I stopped just short of a smile and even, to be perfectly precise, short of a hint of a smile, a preliminary sketch of a smile. If I were to depict myself at that moment, I might show myself with the pencil two fingers from the paper and a large eraser close at hand. But that much was accomplished at least; I'd unclenched my jaws, and I vaguely sensed that my gaze profited from that slight slackening. I don't know just what was in my gaze, a little of that easing of the jaws, no doubt, maybe even a little of the smile that my lips did not really allow themselves to form. In short, I was noticeably ahead of schedule in that way, my eyes a little ahead of my lips. All told, I said to myself, that's not a bad beginning. And since you do have a head start, in your eyes, since the most essential elements of your smile are already there, you can use this time to take in a more global view of this woman. Don't take your eyes off her face, just step back a little. Let your gaze glide, discreetly, or if you like let it linger a little, yes, since you have a head start there, like the hare in the fable. It doesn't matter to her anyway, she's already captured it, your gaze I mean, she's noticed the easing you've introduced, and in a sense she's taking a step back as well, savoring her triumph, so the time has come, now or never, for a fuller picture of what it is that's carrying you off like this, far from the life you thought was yours, desperately hard, wasted, almost over already. Far from Marge as well. And Anne. Far from yourself.

And so, furtively, under the cover of my calm demeanor, I reframed the woman. She wasn't beautiful, as I have said, but incontestably, let me say this before I make her visible, fully visible, she did something for me. Heaven, somehow, at some point, must have conceived her for the express purpose of sending her my way and, I said to myself, there's nothing you can do, faced with such a gift, but accept it. But that's not all, you have to return the favor, too. You're going to have to give, yes, I told myself, as you've given already, of course, except that this time it's the real thing, the one real thing. There has never been another, there will never be another. And now you can take your time. You know just how it will be. The walls can crumble around you, it won't change a thing, a child can drown before your eyes, you won't save it, you won't even have seen it, you'll be somewhere else, you're somewhere else already, in the promise of this woman.

All the same, I observed to myself, this is no time for making plans. You're here, in the moment, with just this one little problem, what to say to her, but that's a detail, you don't care, you're feeling so at ease now that you just might want to swim a quick lap to celebrate, as if it had all happened already, as if there were nothing more to do, nothing but rejoice, nothing but wear yourself out while you're waiting to see her again. Because you've found her, already, she's found you, you can't believe it, no indeed, or rather yes, you do believe it, you're used to it now, you know this woman now, you've always known this is how she would be, not very tall, thin in spite of her stomach, or rather no. Not in spite of her stomach. Because her stomach, this woman's stomach, is in a sense only tacked onto her. Of course you know perfectly well that no wad of kapok, no empty decoy lies beneath that swimsuit. You know that her stomach is a real stomach, and her own. It's simply the way she carries it, before her as it were, along with the child, so that to take that stomach away would be to reduce her existence, certainly, but not her essence, at most it would be to rob her of some ornament, some transitory adjunct from beneath which her grace clearly shows. For while she is not beautiful, she is full of grace, you see, and her stomach, no less than herself, seems some sort of apparition, inexplicable, yes, but pregnant, abiding, demolishing the very incredulity it arouses. You see what I mean.

Yes, I said to myself, I see. Besides, I'd always had a weakness, I must admit, if not for women yearning for the body of their dreams, at least for those who, having no gift for prediction, or sometimes despite their best predictions, sadly observe the discreet, progressive rounding, whether rooted in physical makeup or diet, of a stomach that for several decades a fashion founded on erasure has sought relentlessly to contain. For the ready-to-wear market, seeking only to girdle and shrink all comers, has long distanced itself from the sort of stomach whose convexity I myself have often savored, sometimes with my eyes, more rarely with my hand, which found no less sustenance there than atop a breast or a buttock, such that to my mind those women easily trumped the rest, their asset all the less negligible in that as one neared the pubis a slope began to form, over which the hand slipped in a manner rather akin to gliding downhill, or diving into water, once it had surmounted that soft obstacle that is, to which nothing forbade a return, climbing uphill again, or, sometimes, to which everything obliged it to return, faced with a closure, and lacking a more secret refuge.

It should be clear that at this point, in discovering that woman, and entering into her gaze, and already into her life, it seemed to me, it should be clear that in discovering this woman, whose stomach so graciously eclipsed all others, affirming its own existence in the incomparable mode of the triumphal, I had taken a decisive step. That said, I personally wasn't expecting a child. Not right away at least. Things were obviously changing now, and I could see that it was time to adapt. And, in any case, I was ready. I was going to talk about my apartment a moment ago, and the time has now come to shed some further light on that subject. It was a big apartment, as the reader might recall. And if I had chosen to live in a big apartment, I can say this now, it was also because there would be room for a little one. I say a little one because I want to remain neutral. But the fact is that I was hoping for a girl. I've always yearned for a woman to give me a girl. Because I've long had a horror of little boys, who inevitably turn out wrong. They begin by fighting in the schoolyard and in the final stage become bad colleagues. No, I wanted a girl, in my big apartment, and there was room for her, in her little room. The only thing missing was a woman to give me one, to inspire in me the desire to give her one. Anne wasn't her, no one was her, and now this woman was her, who hadn't, it's true, waited for me to come along before setting things in motion, but who was awaiting me, unless I'd made a serious misjudgment – but that was an eventuality I didn't even consider – to see them through to their conclusion. She was offering me her stomach, now that the process was coming to a close, in order to pass me the fruit, a fruit no doubt scorned by another, what matter, there was nothing calculated in our actions, neither hers nor mine, not mine at least, all I wanted was this woman, now, this illusorily heavy woman, standing there, but in any case not heavy for long, I said to myself, goodness no, surely not very much longer, I repeated to myself, as a matter of fact you'd do well to pick up the pace a bit, this was the woman and none other, then, and I was just what she needed, maybe she was lonely, feeling abandoned, and I was the one she'd cho-

48

sen. For, I must point this out, there were other men, in this pool, other men alone, but I was the one she was staring at, the one she'd allowed to approach her, to have a word with her, among other things, so that I might speak that word to her, and now I was beginning to have some idea of what that word would be, a precise idea, I had yet to formulate it, certainly, but now a surge of confidence came over me, and suddenly I launched in, and I asked her a question, the only one worth asking, I thought, in any case the only one that mattered to me henceforth. The question, that is, of sex. And a few moments later I was telling myself that I'd once again missed a good opportunity to keep my mouth shut.

For all signs, apparently, suggested that the baby would be a boy. At least, she told me with perfect candor, maintaining a smile that I feared did not concern me alone, the sonogram, although not entirely clear, had offered a glimpse of a rather unambiguous blob, a sort of appendage, she said – that word alone was enough to send a shiver down my spine – whose nature her gynecologist could not quite define – I breathed a little more easily – unless it was a thing she then named, the gynecologist I mean, but whose name I cannot repeat here without the harrowing memory of the impression it left on me, spoken by this woman, what's more, with perfect composure, in which I nevertheless thought I detected a trace of delectation.

I'll say this at once: I was crushed. I couldn't understand how this woman, whom I had just chosen, and whom I was perfectly prepared to love – whom I loved already, in fact, I knew it well, that phenomenon, the phenomenon of love, starting up within me, as surely as its object, for her part, was about to bring forth new life – I couldn't understand how here before me she could so coolly envisage the possibility that the child we would be bringing up together might be a boy. No, I simply couldn't understand it, and in the very grips of this uncertainty, I underwent what is no doubt the most astonishing evolution that has ever befallen me.

For, since the thing had already happened, in any event, and as the previous lines have no doubt made clear, the choice that I was then obligated to make was in fact no choice at all. It was an ultimatum that faced me now, with no escape clause through which I might glimpse an unclouded future. This woman, whom I was awaiting, and who was awaiting me as well, judging by her persistent smile, was also awaiting the birth of a baby boy, a fact of which I had not been forewarned, fired back at me out of the blue in response to a question that in spite of its gravity I had intended to be banal, and tailor-made to cement our newborn relationship. In no way could the cordiality of the tone in which I'd posed that question be construed as justifying a response of such violence.

Nevertheless, the deed was done, and as she spread her arms wide on either side of her body, letting her hands drift over the surface of the pool, made choppy by the children's splashings, her palms flat against the water as if to gauge its level, or even to hold it back, or perhaps to test its volume, as if it were a sister in conception, a stomach churned from within by many young lives wriggling in a lapping, liquid chaos, I observed this woman and, I don't consider the word too strong, not too anachronistic, I continued, I continued, I say, to love her, to desire her, to want her. And even now I was beginning to give in, imagining the child, that little boy, yes, beginning to hope that the one who had conceived him was not one of that other crowd, that immense crowd of men contrary to my heart, and soon I was this close to asking her who the father was, what he looked like, and especially how, having left him, she, this woman who had swept me off my feet – or how, having proved unworthy of her, he – might offer this little boy some chance of not ending up like all the rest. Unless, I said to myself, of course, fortunately, it was from her that the boy would derive his every quality, his grace, his sweetness, his strength. And that was the idea, I think, that helped me not to choose, to continue down the path that this woman was clearing for me, a path open to me now, and that allowed me to change the subject, more or less maintaining my composure – the very sign, perceptible to her perhaps, so obvious was it, of my acceptance.

And so I chanced a remark, rather anodyne, concerning the candlepower of ceiling lights, I mean the lights that illuminate swimming pools, those that are covered by a roof, underground, without which all is darkness, and I saw her raise an eye heavenward. For the first time, or nearly so, since our meeting, she wasn't looking at me. And, free of her gaze for the second time, I saw her as I'd first seen her, not yet seeing me, and my first glimpse of her seemed long past now, hours before, or days, as if I were now, unseen, gazing on a woman who, already participating in my life to some extent, had casually chosen to take some time off, to take a break, in no way ominous, from a daily existence that might have been ours.

Then her gaze returned to me, and as she answered, re the lights, that it was surprising they weren't tougher, on the eyes – but it may be, she added, that, unaware of their presence, people not only didn't look at them but in fact didn't even see them, thus protecting themselves from that brilliance through a happy abdication of their awareness – it was then that I thought I saw, but this is only a detail, had become only a detail, ten meters away, Marge.

Obviously, my mind was on other things. One sole idea occupied my thoughts, that it would be a boy, and I was trying to get used to that idea, in spite of everything, as I waited for this woman to bring the child into the world, telling myself that in the end a son, if it was hers, especially so small, as it would be, when it was born, well, there was no way of knowing what my reaction might be; after all, this woman had already brought about a change in me, so why not him too, her son, soon to be spouting that monosexual babble by which every child makes its presence known, and by which we all know how utterly we are undone, all of us, men and women alike, so why not me, and later on when, his hand in mine, I would lead him to school, her son, who would in a sense be mine, then, I said to myself, because I will have taught him, taught him to love women, his mother to begin with, and to beware of men, myself excluded, but also of the girls he would later bring home, that consoled me a bit, the idea that he would bring girls home to me, the link would not be severed, I told myself, and, after all, this may well be the right choice, a son, the best, yes, whereas a girl, have you ever stopped to think that what she'd be bringing home would be men, sooner or later, home to your big apartment, ah, you never thought of that, did you? I said to myself. And so, obviously, when I thought I spotted Marge, coming toward me, my reflex was to disappear, my only thought to hide. And I knew just how to hide in a swimming pool – underwater – but the problem was that I didn't want to hide, on the contrary, I wanted this woman, whose name I had yet to learn, to see me, to go on seeing me, to grow accustomed to the sight of me. In short, this time, the task at hand was not to grasp the branch extended in my direction, thorny or otherwise; the task at hand was to make a decision. And I made it.

I acted as though I hadn't recognized Marge. And, at that very moment, Flore dove. Yes, she was called, or rather went by the name, Flore. I only learned this later, at which time I reflected that in her condition, she really could have covered the entirety of her name, Florence, less suggestive of a symbol, but, I said to myself, we'll go with the symbol, and in any case that's her name, so Flore it is, my life, and that's that, no point in discussing it further.

I even began to like the name.

In the meantime, Flore was diving. Which is to say that, uniting and extending her arms before her, she sank into the pool without visible transition, as if drawn toward the bottom, then seemed to stabilize, like a skiff on its keel, while like a prow she clove the water with her two cyclically joined hands and headed off at a leisurely clip, her little feet – which I only then discovered – sometimes skimming the surface as if at one extreme of a powerful rocking motion that she was not entirely able to contain.

In sum, she was abandoning me.

Facing Marge.

Whom she surely didn't know.

Although, I said to myself, the coincidence is troubling.

I launched myself into the water after Flore.

I caught up to her where the shallow water turned deep, a boundary marked by a sign hung from a sagging chain stretched across the pool.

We slipped beneath the sign – deep end, it read, 1.5 meters –

and from behind my goggles, I cast Flore a sidelong glance to signify that I too was here, at this pool, to swim.

In other words, that from my point of view nothing in any way unusual was happening.

This was our first trip together.

At the far edge of the deep end, Flore stopped and stood upright, her shoulders emerging from the water.

That was how I learned of the existence of the pedestal. Twenty centimeters high, submerged under 1.3 meters of water, more or less, it offered the swimmers a breather.

We breathed.

Now I saw Marge cast off in turn.

Heading in our direction.

I asked Flore if she was tired.

She gave me a half-smile, and I told her I'd be back.

I've always said that to women. Even for a trip to the bathroom.

Maybe that's why they always leave me.

But I wasn't afraid that Flore would leave me.

On the way, I passed by Marge, who didn't look at me.

Me neither.

I arrived at the far edge of the shallow end reflecting that Marge didn't seem to be looking for me very hard.

She made an about-face at the opposite end of the pool, and Flore set off alongside her.

Now they were both coming at me.

I couldn't bear to turn my back on Flore.

So I faced Marge.

It was her. Ten years had gone by, just like that, serenely, one after another, none of them, by all appearances, having stood out as unusually tempestuous. Marge was the only really beautiful woman I'd ever known – a simple matter of chance – and she still was, still beautiful, and even more so than ever.

But I'd stopped loving her long before.

And then something remarkable happened, or so at least it seemed to me, something that truly strained credulity.

Marge didn't recognize me.

I didn't go so far as to remove my goggles and give her a chance to see her mistake. And as far as I was concerned, there was no great merit in my having recognized her through her goggles and my own. I never forget a face. People can change, ten years can go by, and I spot them straight off. I'm attentive to others that way.

It disturbed me somewhat that Marge hadn't recognized me, when for my part I had put a name, hers, to those openly unretiring lips, one, the lower, underlining the other almost to the point of effacing it, so flamboyantly did it pout; to that nose, straight, with a slight upward tilt to the barrier between the nostrils, accentuated by the goggles; to the discreet inward curve at the bottom of her face, nudging what was at that point a flawless oval toward the more common but also more sensual figure of a circle. It disturbed me somewhat, but, I told myself, it really shouldn't surprise you. We must of course note that, against all expectations, Marge did come to the meeting she'd arranged with you, but for all you know, she was planning to come here anyway, to this pool. To work on her form. Whereas this other woman here never arranged to meet up with you. And she came anyway. And now she's coming back. Toward you. With Marge, yes. Who is now, however, going away again.

For Marge had set off back toward the deep end, while Flore, breathless, resumed her position at my flank, as if returning from an absence. An absence to which we had mutually agreed. I didn't know what to do about Marge, her presence, after ten years, the great slab of a life grown distant from mine offered up to me here, unembellished, in the form of a ripened body, a gaze grown unable to see me. A fiasco, certainly. But a fiasco without consequences, not even worth counting, even if I were still counting, which I wasn't. I no longer counted. I no longer existed. Happily, I was no longer inside myself. And, hypertension aside, I was feeling inclined to believe that the era now dawning might bring me some repose.

Flore too, in a sense, was aspiring to a little rest. Her fatigue seemed to be calling for a departure in the coming minutes. She stretched out her arms again, laterally, once more laying her hands against the water, but in her gesture, this time, were the premises of a conclusion that immediately put me on guard.

Fortunately, Flore was not only tired but also spoke of her tiredness. I'm tired, she said, specifically, and for some time that sentence remained in my mind as what it was equivalent to, retained for some time the character of an admission. I've always been moved, ever since, whatever the context, whenever I've heard it spoken. Even if a man speaks those words to evoke some benign hypoglycemia, unlikely to cut him down, I find myself aflutter like a schoolgirl. There are sentences like that in life, with a meaning locked away inside, that you have to find your way around.

So Flore wanted to leave. That was what she was telling me. And, to be sure, it sometimes happens that a woman indicating such a desire simultaneously informs you that she is leaving you. But this was not Flore's meaning. She was saying I'm tired, and her gaze, more languid than her words, added this, which constituted the full sense of the utterance: Let's go.

And it would not be too much to say that we went.

It all happened a little strangely, it's true, for Flore, expecting me to, as it were, complete her sentence with a sentence of my own, or a gesture, was still testing the waters of the pool, her two hands lying flat on the surface, as if, having simply decided that we would go, that this was how it had to be, with or without my help, she had resigned herself to waiting for the level to rise until the water itself hoisted us up and washed us ashore. But I took it upon myself to accelerate the process, suggesting that we leave and find a café for a drink.

It was of course slightly ridiculous, and even regressive, since we were together already, to suggest to this woman standing half-naked in a pool, with me half-naked beside her, that we part only to meet up again fully dressed, and on dry land yet, with, as the sole reminder of the water in which we once stood, a little liquid, absurdly less liquid, sitting before us in a glass into which we would plunge, at best, nothing more than a plastic swizzle stick girdled with a lemon round. But my proposal was met with no dismay. And so we parted at the top of the ladder, making for our respective showers, agreeing to reunite at the hairdryers by the front desk. Coin-operated, again.

I let myself fall slightly behind, once she'd forded the footbath on her way to the showers, intending to catch up by dressing more speedily, which seemed only likely. Two steps away from the footbath, on the men's side, I paused for one last glance at the pool, where Marge was continuing her maneuvers.

The surprising thing, I observed, is that she doesn't even seem to be looking for me. This seemed somehow implausible, and I wondered whether it really was her after all. I had of course accounted for the passage of time in my attempt to identify her, and in spite of everything, it was indeed her face, perceptibly changed, that I thought I'd seen. But what I thought of as different, and attributed to age, might very well be what, in a woman other than Marge, was the very emblem of her identity, whereas what I had thought I'd recognized in Marge could, in another woman, have come as the result of a change, or even a rejuvenation, assuming of course that between two women there can exist more than a resemblance.

In any event, I watched this woman, Marge or no, swimming off toward the deep end as one receding into the distance, her face slowly fading from sight, as if space, as if the gap this woman was creating between herself and me, physically, standing in for the span of time she had lived without me, as if that space, growing with her every stroke, were slowly becoming the erasure of a memory. And the only sign of recognition sent my way as I left the environs of the pool came from the man who had reinserted my clasp. He waved from the far end of the deep water, perched on the pedestal, one arm broadly motioning, and this left me for a moment reflecting on the strange camaraderie that brings men together, sometimes, on the grounds that, in the face of some adversity, no matter how minimal, they have struggled.

I had some trouble with my socks. The feet are quite probably the least easily dried of all body parts, no doubt because man, when denied the possibility of sitting – as was my case in this booth, whose little bench I had laden with my belongings, loath as I was to dampen them by laying them on the floor, itself dampened already – because man, I say, has no access to the soles of his feet with his towel except by turns, and even then only at the price of a precarious one-legged stance. And, with the floor already dampened, I was furthermore obligated, having approximately dried my left foot, to hold it suspended in midair as I attempted to thread my sock over it, prolonging still further my reliance on the right, a task in which I failed only once, to be sure, but once was enough to force me, my left foot having somehow plummeted earthward and encountered the puddle over which I balanced, to begin the process all over again. Thankfully, the sock was not yet in place. But my greatest difficulty was not with that foot.

For now, standing upright on my left foot, over which I had finally fit my sock and, following in its footsteps if I may, my shoe, I succeeded without too much difficulty in keeping the right foot in the air, bare, but on this latter foot, alas still too wet to be sheathed with ease, the second sock, reaching the halfway point, refused to go on, leaving the closed end hanging limp as I tugged at the open end in a vain struggle to get the thing on one way or another. Several precious seconds went by with no change in the situation, and soon I had no choice but to doff the sock entirely and gather it up in my hands such that the closed end, acting as a buffer for my toes, might allow me,

61

slowly unfurling, to hoist the open end to the appropriate height, which is to say that of my ankle.

And with all this, I have said nothing of the heels, the foot's and the sock's, which I never did bring into perfect alignment. In short, time was passing, and I was growing ever later.

I hurried toward the hairdryers, still convinced, in my persistent euphoria, that I would find Flore faithfully awaiting our meeting. But I didn't find her. I remained resolutely unperturbed, assuming that she'd simply fallen even farther behind than I, that she wouldn't leave me hanging here, as I might ordinarily have expected, and when she did appear, I was close to a breakdown, but I soon recovered.

I did my best to conceal my emotion, believing it absolutely essential to do so, for Flore might perhaps have thought it odd that I should be so utterly undone by such a trifling delay. She, at least, seemed to find this all perfectly normal, being here with me, even after a separation of twenty long minutes. She was simply with me again, naturally, and, I noted, she seemed to see our reunion less as a renewal of our acquaintance than as a resumption of our relationship where it had left off, as if our brief time together had already acquired the status of something definitive. I took the liberty of rejoicing at this, and as she dried herself beneath a nozzle fixed into the wall, briskly tossing her head, as women do on such occasions, sending a surprisingly voluminous mass of hair flying this way and that, I looked on discreetly, almost happy already, reckoning that the one and only thing my full happiness now required was a little time, always a little more time, of course, from now on, with her, anywhere and at any price.

(Any price that didn't involve money, that is. I had little, and no more to come in the future. But this was of no concern to me now. I wasn't thinking about that side of things.)

This was also my first glimpse of Flore fully dressed. A woman I scarcely knew. I tried to avoid eyeing her too overtly in this state, newly draped in one of those dresses tailored for women in her condition, but the fact is that her dress did not seem particularly tailored to me, or not enough. Once past the breasts, it abruptly bulged outward, then resumed its vertical fall, like a bundle of clothes she carried before her, along with the child, at some small remove from herself, as if to show it the way, the dress I mean, probably toward the closet or even more probably a secondhand clothes shop, to be handed off once the child was out. It was this ephemeral aspect that struck you most of all, for in that dress Flore herself seemed to evoke, between the lines, the woman she would become, wrapped in that diaphanous drapery, leaving little to the imagination, what was and what would be, where she was concerned at least, for myself, I wasn't hazarding any guesses, it was already enough, quite a lot, that this woman was here with me, on the verge of childbirth, as if to offer me the fruit, but I wasn't asking for that, no, not right away at least, I can wait, I told myself, although it would be nice to have some idea how long the wait might be, to project a date, clearly soon, though, I said to myself, but all the same, she must know when, some vague inkling, and suddenly, my dithering at an end, I came out and asked her.

As I was telling myself that this time I'd gone too far, Flore, tending to her hair with sweeping strokes of her brush, gave me an evasive answer in which, purely at random, I caught the word fifteen. The word had floated vaguely to the surface of her sentence. Perhaps she'd half-swallowed or mumbled it, and only a bit of it had poked through to the top, or perhaps I'd deduced it from some more general sense, from her tone, I don't quite remember; in any case, we were soon out in the street searching for a café, conversing without reserve, even venturing into the question of the first name, the child's – un-

63

imaginable to me, since it was a boy, but, to my surprise, to her as well – which left me an opening to talk to Flore about names in general, about my ignorance of hers, whereas she surely knew what it was, inevitably, unlike the child's, and perhaps she would be so kind as to communicate it to me. That would be a beginning, I said. As for me, it's Luc, but that doesn't really matter, they usually call me Gavarine.

As we made our way, I knew not where, no doubt the café we were looking for – but we'd dropped that question, and we passed by several such establishments without mention, which were closed anyway – Flore, who evidently had no particular interest in my gym bag, nonetheless asked what I was carrying in my briefcase.

Not what I had in it, but what I was carrying in it. As if in her eyes my briefcase, not unlike herself, as she cautiously advanced, a little behind herself, with short strides, toes outward, conforming to a choreography whose classicism in no way limited its fascination, easily the rival of any rarity, as if my briefcase, I was saying, must perforce contain something extraordinary, and as if, that day, by that briefcase, I was encumbered only for specific and even curious reasons, reasons at least that intrigued her to such an extent that, encouraged by the burgeoning familiarity of our exchanges, she felt at ease to make inquiries.

What I then felt was a mingled sensation, astonishment vying with gratitude, both giving way in the end to the awareness of a vanity. I really hadn't expected this woman, the first to have displayed any real preoccupation with my briefcase, to concern herself with such matters; or rather, that briefcase, which so intrigued this woman I was beginning to consider my own, no longer preoccupied me. Nevertheless, it was empty, I remembered, and I hesitated to say so. It was too much, too long a story, and so I lied.

Nothing, nothing, I said.

And the sense that I had somehow spoken a truth deceived

me only momentarily, after the fact, in the wake of a semantic echo. Not so Flore, whom I had convinced with these same words that my briefcase contained something I preferred to keep to myself. It seems quite clear to me, of course, that this was not an attempt to conceal my shame at carrying an empty briefcase, a shame not all that burning, really, since I had my reasons for doing so, not entirely ill-founded. No, what I was attempting to conceal was my shame at having secrets, secrets from her, when my greatest desire was that nothing come between us that might act as an obstacle. Having lied so flagrantly, or having at least so flagrantly avoided this subject, I now had to introduce another, and as I searched for something suitable, Flore, apparently undismayed by my excessive evasiveness, once again spoke to me of the pool, in such a way, I sensed, as to suggest that we might see each other again there, on some other occasion.

I must confess that I found the proposition scandalous. The pool was where we had come from, it was far away now, far from me at least, and, I presumed, far from both of us, far behind, for now Flore and I were moving forward, now and forevermore, toward a place without pools, without Marge, without Anne Lebedel to drive me into the arms of women who go to pools, in addition to which, in addition to my lack of desire to see Marge again, I'm really not all that fond of pools. I was glad to have met Flore at a pool, in fact: that much at least was taken care of, out of the way, and I wouldn't have to undergo the experience again, and now Flore, I gathered, as if something had not already taken place, something between us, something irreversible, now Flore was suggesting that we revert to just such a place in the near future.

No, I said, therefore. I don't usually go to that pool. I don't go to any pool. I'm not that fond of pools. But, and I don't know how possible this might be, I'd like to be fond of you, and anyway I already do, I said, I already like being fond of you, but, I added, eager to make myself fully understood, I'm not all that fond of pools. Or of the past in general, I went on to add, but I told myself that as remarks go that last one was not particularly clear, in the current context. With this I fell silent, thinking back on what I'd just said. You are completely insane, I told myself, or more precisely you lack even the most elementary sense of prudence; it must in fact be the case that you take some sort of pleasure in behaving like a complete imbecile. You just don't know what to do with yourself when you're not acting like an imbecile, do you? But no, you're right: just in case you might still have some small chance of not ruining everything, you never know, why not just blow it all to hell right away? It's better than being happy.

So what were you doing there? said Flore.

For she was speaking to me. Responding to my words. I had indeed said something, back at the beginning of my sentence, just what I couldn't quite remember, I vaguely recalled that it had something to do with pools, oh yes, it's coming back to me now, I don't go to them, I'd said, so what was I doing there today, yes, it's a reasonable question, I said to myself, this woman is going to drive me mad with her way of catching nothing but the details, but no, you idiot, you should be grateful, she's giving you a chance, offering it up on a silver platter. So say something, anything, your shower isn't working, say. That's it, your shower isn't working. No?

I suppose.

My shower isn't working, I said.

Blank.

It's mostly for the shower, I resumed. I needed a shower. I don't know if you've noticed, but public baths have become

67

a good deal harder to find nowadays. You know, those tiled buildings, even tiled on the outside.

I added gestures to my words. Summoning up my memories, admittedly sparse, and hastily fitting them together, I endeavored to reconstruct the facade of a public bathhouse.

That won me a smile. A small one. I didn't know quite what to make of it. Anyway, I said to myself, as long as she finds you amusing.

And tomorrow? said Flore.

Tomorrow? I said.

Yes, tomorrow, Flore said. You won't bathe?

A street opened up on the right, and I briefly thought of hurtling down the sidewalk and disappearing into the distance.

Yes, I will. I know a plumber, as it happens. There is as it happens a plumber in my life. He should come by sometime today.

In any case, said Flore, I won't be going to the pool again.

Oh, I said.

I didn't entirely understand. Unless this was to be the end of our relationship, now that we'd passed the crossroads where I'd failed to disappear, which I must now take steps to do. The usual thing, in other words. Although I was a little out of practice. I squeezed the handle of my briefcase hard.

So what if I'd gone back? I said.

To the pool?

Yes, I said. You wouldn't have been there.

You wouldn't have gone back, said Flore. You wouldn't have gone back because I wouldn't have asked you to. But I wanted to know if you would go back, if I did ask you to.

And you still want to know? I said.

Yes, she said.

Yes, I said.

But I'm not asking you to, she said.

68

Right, I said.

I'm going home to my brother's in the Corrèze for the delivery, she said. Tomorrow.

She seemed to expect this to surprise me. But it didn't surprise me. I was ready for anything. Something in my manner must have given her a false impression. A trace of tension in my face, no doubt.

On the 9:05 train, she added.

What number? I said.

I was going to put myself out. Because the heavens were opening. No. A window. A window in a railway car. Unless she'd reserved an aisle seat.

Wait a minute, she said.

She looked through her bag. We'd come to a second intersection. The neighborhood was built on a slope. Nothing much to see in the cross streets, and before us all the shops were closed. Farther on, lower down, much the same. No reason not to stay where we were. It was nice, standing there on the sidewalk.

She showed me her ticket.

She gave me a moment to read it over.

It was enchanting.

I handed it back.

Would you allow me to accompany you? I said.

Yes, she said. But that wouldn't be reasonable.

We looked at each other.

I never said it would, I said.

Let me tell you something, she said. I wouldn't stop you. If it's no bother.

Don't be ridiculous, I said. There's one question, though. I'd like to know.

Yes?

We weren't moving.

If you're glad, I said.

Yes, she said.

Glad about what, I didn't ask: me accompanying her to the train, or accompanying her on the train, or spending the rest of our lives together with the little one? A small uncertainty hung in the air on that point.

But it was too late. Our conversation was rolling along nicely now, and I had no desire to push my way back uphill again.

What mattered most was that I could find no reason not to go. Not that I looked for one. There was no time for that. Reflection was the last thing I needed. What I needed was her. And she was leaving.

We have to find a café, she said.

Yes, I said. Of course.

I didn't move. I looked at her.

I couldn't see what use a café might be to us now.

She could.

I really have to find a café, she said.

Right, I said.

We resumed our descent. At the end of the street, a café appeared. Once inside, Flore vanished into the toilets. I ordered two fruit juices. One yellow, one pink.

I have to go, she said when she came back.

I would have loved to know where. But it was a different question that was now resolved: I would not be accompanying her to the station. Getting to the station was her affair. There were her bags, it's true. And in her condition, of course. Unless, I said to myself, she has someone else to accompany her there. That would be irksome. Not that I had any claim over her. Until the next day. 9:05, she'd told me. I'd seen it written down, too, in black and white. So I wasn't dreaming. All the same, she was leaving awfully suddenly. Now, I mean. We'd had so little time to talk. But I tried to look on the bright side of her departure. I couldn't imagine any other way we could say see you tomorrow. I couldn't very well ask her back to my place, having lost my keys, in addition to which I wouldn't have dared. And I didn't want to anyway. Nor to go to her place. Besides, she hadn't asked me. Stay a little longer, I said.

No, she said, I really have to be on my way.

Her way where? That I would have given anything to know.

Just because it's happening so fast, I told myself, that doesn't mean it isn't real.

It's because it's real, I said to myself, that it's happening so fast. The one is the proof of the other.

At any rate, tomorrow I leave.

In any case.

Excuse me.

Yes?

Another pineapple juice.

Thank you.

Then I went home.

That's what I was about to say.

That's what I was thinking at the time. You have to go home to find any real peace.

So then I went back to the hotel. I was in no mood to linger. The city had nothing to offer me, as long as this day was not the next. Only evening tempted me, with its proximity to night. In my room, I advanced toward evening as best I could. I skirted the walls, first one, then another, assured myself that there was indeed a door within the third, kept my distance from the last, against which my bed was nestled. Then I went downstairs to the telephone. No messages on my answering machine. Neither from Anne nor from Marge. Marge was more troubling. But I wasn't troubled. Maybe she thought I hadn't come. Funny.

I went to bed early, got up late, almost fell asleep at dawn, decided to shave instead. I'd bought some disposable razors on my way back to the hotel. And some clothes. And I still had my gym bag.

72

I shaved from left to right. The effect of confidence, no doubt, intermingled with haste. I didn't usually shave from left to right. Or right to left. I shaved a little on the right, or the left, then a little on the left, or the right. Symmetrically. The upper left cheek, then the upper right. And so on. That way, I used to tell myself, should some cataclysm send you scrambling into the street, you'll have nothing to worry about. No one will think you haven't shaved. They'll think you began, that morning, to trim your beard. Or that you're growing a goatee. I always saved my chin for last.

But not this time. I shaved briskly, but serenely. Unafraid of earthquakes, unafraid of exploding gas lines.

I now had two hours in front of me before I would approach the ticket windows in the train station. I only killed one. It put up a good defense. Defiant was that hour, and arrogant. Your day begins with me, it said. I'd gladly move on, make myself a little later, but that's out of my hands; it's my nature. So it's all up to you. Come on, defend yourself. Fight back, if you're so tough. Go ahead and try. Distract yourself. See if I go by.

It went by. My strength was spent. Faced with the second hour, the eighth in normal time, I threw in the towel. I left the room and headed for the station.

I stayed twenty minutes ahead of schedule. I bought my ticket, then made for the departures board. Too early for the platform number to be listed. No sign of Flore. Nothing odd about that, I said to myself. So she isn't early. Ten minutes later, I began to wonder if she would be on time. Five minutes more, and I was serene again. Finally a normal situation, I said to myself. She won't come. She never intended to come. All the same, I ruminated, I'd rather she came. I'd rather go away with her. What will I do all alone in V——— without her? And only five thousand francs to my name?

Not that I was counting on Flore for money. On the contrary. I would gladly have given her all I had left. Besides, I couldn't imagine what I would do with five thousand francs all on my own. Apart from survive. A little. Maybe that wouldn't be so bad. Survive somewhere else. Somewhere other than here. Here I'd done all I could.

At three minutes before departure time, I was anxious. No, that's not the word. I was losing my mind. I seized the elbow of anyone within reach. Have you seen a woman, I began. I described her. Don't worry, they said to me. You won't have any trouble spotting her. I came close to lashing out.

I leapt into the train. I don't know where she'd come from, but there was Flore. I hadn't spotted her. Incredible. Unless she'd deliberately avoided me. No. She gave me a little smile. Conspiratorial. In what, I wondered. There was a man sitting next to her.

He was laughing. They were both laughing. They'd been laughing together before I came in. A trace of their laughter lingered on their faces. Even Flore's smile, I told myself, is in all likelihood no more than a remainder. A remainder of her laugh. A subsiding. The tail end of the event. I board this train, where she was laughing with this man, and now she isn't laughing anymore. Me neither.

I found an empty spot, seven meters away, and hoisted my bag into the rack above the seat. Train 6045, I heard, doors are now closing, departure in one minute. Fine, I said to myself.

Let's be off.

My seat faced hers. The train began to roll. We were both in aisle seats, and I couldn't see the man. Her, I could see. Listening, by the look of it. She turned her head a little to the left. Toward him. Then looked at me. I looked at her. Unable to express anything with my gaze. She, with hers, on the other hand. A tenderness. So that's how it is, I said to myself. A nightmare. The very one you used to dream of, maybe.

But no, I said to myself. That's just the seat the man reserved. And there was more than tenderness in that gaze. Behind it, there was a questioning. A questioning of the emptiness in mine. Or rather of the questioning, in mine, of hers. That man is the problem. What I need to do is summon up the courage to change places. Ask someone sitting alone to take my place. And leave me his, or hers. Because I wasn't alone. A man sat reading next to me. What I needed, then, was to ask someone sitting alone to take my seat, leaving me his, or hers, along with the adjoining empty seat, and for what exactly? So that I could invite Flore to come and join me, when clearly she's with this character and hasn't made the slightest effort to come and join me. And there she sits, laughing with him. This is going to take some thought, I said to myself.

Beyond the windowpanes, the suburbs were drawing to a close. The houses gradually receded from the tracks. Became chateaux, farm buildings. Lakes appeared amid the greenery. A road snaked into the distance.

Right, I said to myself. So that's that. The train is moving. I'm on my way. Maybe this is going to be my own journey. Mine alone. This woman, looking at me, inexplicably, sitting next to that man and laughing with him, this is all perfectly normal. She's seeing me on my way to hell. Holding my hand, from a distance. There, she's telling me, this is where you're going. Without me. It'll be hard, I know, so I'm sticking around for a while. Although that's probably a mistake. Too sensitive for my own good, if you ask me. Men have always had that effect on me. Not pity, no. Sympathy. The way they throw themselves against the wall, again and again. I can't help it, it moves me.

I almost fell asleep. I tried. That way, I told myself, I might have a nice surprise when I open my eyes again. The man will have disappeared. And in the place of my neighbor, my neighbor who's just folded up his newspaper, her. You can always dream.

But I was afraid to close my eyes. Afraid she might seize the opportunity to disappear. Although that would make things clearer, at least. No. It was better this way. It was better to see her. More complicated. Complications, I said to myself, that's all I have left. That and my briefcase. I'd brought it with me. The last vestige of my prudence.

Then Flore stood up.

She came toward me.

Every two meters, she steadied herself against a seatback.

She leaned against mine.

Hello, she said.

I felt able to respond. By which I mean that even as she deprived me of it, me there in my seat, her leaning over it and me slumped down in it, transfixed, no, slumped, yes, undone, suddenly, she gave me the strength I needed.

Hello, I said.

That's not a bad start, I thought.

A kind of calm descended over me. It's not so hard, I told myself, to be reborn. I felt naked, lightened of my cares. I was coming back to life. All perfectly transparent, in the end. That obvious fact, which I never seem to see, never. That someone exists, somewhere. Someday. And that that someone is today. Here. And she was there yesterday too. That proves it.

He's getting off at the next stop, Flore told me.

She was leaning over me. I felt her breath. Or imagined it. In any case, she was murmuring. She's murmuring, I said to myself, she's murmuring this to me. That he's getting off. Breathily. Whence my mistake. It's not her breath I'm feeling. It's that sen-

76

tence, the meaning of the sentence she's just offered up to me. That man means nothing to me. Doesn't exist. Come and join me after the next stop.

She now said.

Then she headed off toward the toilets. I watched the man stand up, collect his bags, and step into the aisle, along with a number of others. The train braked. Five-minute stop. The man got off. All very ordinary, of course. But still. Flore came back, passed by me. She touched my arm, returned to her seat. I could have ripped my arm off. You don't need two arms. One good arm, fine, and the other one, the one she'd just touched, in formaldehyde. On the mantelpiece. In my big apartment. When she leaves me.

I stood up, came to join her. She was still waiting for me. In the window seat now. I sat down beside her, beside the aisle. Now I couldn't really see her anymore.

You should have come over, she said. And said something. He would have given you his seat.

Her voice. I haven't yet mentioned her voice. Later.

You wouldn't have laughed as much, I said.

I see, she said.

Peripheral vision is a wonderful thing. I glimpsed a corner of her smile from where I sat. I'll talk about her smile too.

I didn't feel like laughing, she said. It was him. Laughing doesn't mean that much to me. Sometimes you laugh because there's nothing else to do. Besides, as you see, I'm not laughing anymore, she said, still smiling that same smile. I don't like laughing. It makes me nervous. I laugh because I'm nervous. Always. But with you, you make me calm.

No, I said, that's impossible. Absolutely impossible. I'm extremely tense. You don't make me calm at all. Or only with great difficulty. You make me calm with great difficulty.

That's better than nothing, she said.

And I don't know any funny stories, I said.

We're not going to fight, she said, we've only got an hour. Then we'll be at the station, and my brother will be there. His name is Jean. He's going to be surprised to see you.

It would have been nice to sleep. Now that I was by her side, that would have been ideal. Then wake up to see her brother. Since I was going to see him. I hadn't known that. I didn't know anything. I told her so. I don't know anything. You're accompanying me, she said. Yes, I said. But how far? I didn't add. Ah, she said softly. Aaaah.

She held her stomach. I would gladly have held her stomach a bit myself. Or her hand on her stomach. Facing me, my ex-neighbor, the man with the newspaper, had moved over to the aisle seat. Watching me, inquisitive. I cast him a glance. That's right, my glance said. This woman is about to give birth. That's why I came and joined her. It's my job. I watch over women who are about to give birth, in trains, and at the first contraction, bang, I leave my seat and come over. I put my hand on their stomachs. The pay's not good, but well.

Are you going to be all right? I asked.

Yes, she told me. It's over now. But it's getting close. The delivery was supposed to be in a week.

And now? I said.

Now, she said, I think actually it's going to be now. When I get off the train. I want to go to the hospital, she said. Right away.

She held back a sob. Her face wrinkled up. Her mouth. I'll talk about her mouth. Then everything hardened. Somewhere on her, unthinking, I put my hand. It met hers. I left it there. Flore went limp.

I need help, she told me.

78

Yes, I said.

More than anything, she needed someone. And I was only me. And now my hand on hers had lost its effect. Once contact was established, our temperatures melded. Contact, as we all know, is felt primarily through a difference in temperature. I took away my hand to let it cool. Then put it back. Hers had cooled even more. I warmed it for her. And so, with our two hands resting on her stomach, one atop the other, in the slight swaying of the train, we held to some kind of course. I said nothing more about the child. It was too close. Our fears were conjoined in the silence. The countryside was growing hillier. One line of hills blocked the view of others, fading into a pale dimness far away. The sky was white.

Every now and then I asked Flore for an update. It's OK, she told me. I took my hand away. I waited for her to ask for it back. She didn't. She stood up and made her way toward the toilets, clinging again to the seatbacks. Again I asked if she was all right. Yes, she said. Right, I said. I said no more, I didn't dare. Didn't know. The countryside rolled past, for no one. I waited for the next contraction. Let her suffer, I said to myself. I'm not asking for much. A clenching of the jaws. A gritting of the teeth. I waited.

Slowly, I mean quickly, much more quickly than one might suppose from this slowness – purely illusory, in point of fact – the time passed. Then she took my hand. We were pulling into V——— . I squeezed her hand. No, she said. You can take my bags instead. She took her stomach in the meantime. With both hands. Are you going to be all right? I said. Can you stand up?

Come on, she said. Don't overdo it. It goes away. When it goes away, it goes away. It's gone away.

I followed her down the aisle. Straps over my shoulders, my

hands full of handles, I bumped the seats as I passed. She climbed down on her own, clinging to the banister. I caught up with her. We followed arrows. There were people waiting for other people. There he is, she said.

A man was coming toward us. I didn't take the time to see him. I walked ahead of Flore, went to meet him, spoke a few words about the woman behind me. His sister, yes. We've got to hurry, I added. Yes, he said to me. Of course. Pleased to meet you, he went on to say. My name is Jean.

Jean, then, steering us briskly toward the exit, simultaneously attempted to shake my hand and relieve me of a bag, or even two, and as he delivered me we briefly locked pinkies, the latter still manipulable despite our respective prehensions, in a modest sort of way, limited to the first phalanges. He was a tall man, and big, more so than me, surpassing me in the three known dimensions by a half-head, quarter-shoulder, and easily third of a stomach, all this with a sort of placidity unsullied by any discernible self-satisfaction. Talkative, too, and in a register so diverse that before we had reached his vehicle, I already knew, in some detail, the history of his family, the situation in the Horn of Africa, and the rate, seasonally variable, as he explained, of his gasoline consumption. He consumed less in the winter. In Africa, things were heating up. His family had a long history.

We started off gently, then picked up speed, nonetheless taking care to spare Flore and the brakes when we approached a red light. We spoke little, except for Jean. I personally had nothing to say, not about my own situation at least, which I found too uncertain to convey even to myself. I wasn't sure what I was supposed to be doing there, and I was reluctant to get Jean, who hardly needed the encouragement, started up again. As for Flore, even in the absence of her brother, our exchanges had been so sparse that I was beginning to think we really should try to get acquainted sometime, before it was too late. Which is to say before the birth. The prospect of an ever-expanding number of intermediaries in our relationship was beginning to disturb me. And I was realizing that it was already too late for us ever to be alone together. I thought I was meeting a woman, and it turns out I can scarcely open my mouth without entering into a relationship with a member of her family.

Flore complained only once, during her third contraction. She looked at her watch. In the front seat, as dictated by custom but also by necessity, she slumped, out of sight. Jean continued to broaden my knowledge of his tastes, his peeves, his phobias. First and foremost, a fear of empty spaces. In conversation particularly.

Rarely did he make mention of Flore. I concluded that beneath his extroversion lay a certain discretion, rather anemic, which he proved extremely reluctant to coddle.

The hospital was not as distant from the station as my fears had led me to believe. Soon we were there. We emerged from the car in no particular order. Jean, then Flore. I brought up the rear. In the entryway, Flore hesitated. Come on, you've been here before, Jean remarked. I don't remember, Flore moaned. We read signs. Yellow Zone, one said. Emergency Obstetrics, the other explained. Larger than the first. Of an imposing size, in fact. Wait for me at the front desk, I suggested. You never know with hospitals. Tell Flore to sit down, I slipped to Jean. There's no point in her following arrows if they aren't the right ones. I'll go and see. I'll be back.

I wanted to take matters into my own hands. I couldn't speak, but I could act. Distinguish myself by my conduct. That was important to me. I was happy to be of use. I needed it.

In the end, I only followed one arrow. Enormous, like the sign. It pointed me down a hallway, where I found nothing more of interest to read. Only a few cramped little labels – Admissions, Billing, I read – pasted to panes of glass whose perforations aerated only empty cubicles. Next to my big arrow, these were very minor works. I only had eyes for my arrow.

Which led me to another. More modest in size, and tilted upward. I raised my eyes. A door stood before me. Tall. Closed. More than that, stated a hand-lettered sign of what seemed to me enormous significance. No entry, it said. Please go around.

I set out to go around. To my right, another door. Open, yes, but giving onto a row of telephone booths. Yet another to my left, also open, and through it a staircase plunging into the basement. I began my descent, not without caution. The bare surface of the floor was flaking away here and there. No paint coated the walls. Here too there was something to read, an unframed inscription submitted to the public eye by a hasty and vindictive hand at an uncertain date. Anne-Marie Lafertigue is a bitch, it informed the passerby. I'll make her pay, it went on to say a little farther on, a little lower down, where the stairway opened onto something like a basement.

At the bottom I turned right, for, I said to myself, if what I am doing is going around, having turned left through that door, I must now face right. I passed by some gigantic garbage cans full of septic waste. A room then came into view, rather vast, rather like a parking lot, minus the bituminous surface, with monitoring devices set out in rows. There was something bleak about it, a feeling of insidious decay. I turned right again, discovered what appeared to be a changing room, where a woman was undressing. She was taking off her surgical smock. She didn't see me. She was having difficulty removing the smock. Then she sank. To her knees. Collapsed.

Hey! I shouted.

I was forced to kneel down. She seemed to be unconscious. I took her wrist, shook it; it fell earthward. I raised an eyelid, same thing. Next I gave her a vigorous overall shake and, however slight the chance of being heard, firmly asked where I might find Emergency. Obstetrics, I specified.

None of which meant anything to her. Utter indifference, but of a vaguely mocking sort, I thought. Nevertheless, I didn't take the time to slap her. I headed back to the stairs, climbed to the top, exited the basement, entered another staircase, the first I came to, and climbed that as well, heading for other floors in hopes of discovering someone. No one. It was clean, though. Right, I said to myself. Then I saw someone. A man. I'm looking for Emergency, I said. Obstetrics. Ah, he answered. For what reason?

I didn't want to kill anyone. Calmly, I explained that it was for my wife. Once he'd pointed me in the right direction, not the same direction as before, fortunately, I informed my informant that a woman lay in the basement. One of your colleagues, I suppose. Taking off her smock.

Wait a minute, said the man. What did you say?

Nothing, I said. Just that a woman has fainted in the basement.

And I left him standing there. With persistence, I did eventually reach Emergency Obstetrics. The door was locked, albeit equipped with a buzzer and a small sign. Press the former, said the latter. I buzzed. I waited. Someone came and opened the door. Yes, what is it? I was asked.

I repeated myself. Here, where pathways allowed themselves to be followed only with difficulty, where doors rarely opened, I was growing used to speaking of my wife. Taking to it quite readily, actually. And my interlocutors as well, it seemed. That, at least, they never disputed. But, I was told, when you come here for a delivery, as a rule, you don't go to Emergency. You go to Obstetrics.

I didn't take time to ask the woman at the door just what, in that case, might be the purpose of Emergency Obstetrics.

I asked only where Obstetrics was to be found. Next to Emer-

84

gency, she told me. Emergency Obstetrics? I inquired. Of course, she told me. And so I made my way to Emergency Obstetrics, and with some difficulty found Obstetrics, just next door, it's true, but unindicated by any sign. I pushed the door open for a look. No one to be seen at the front desk of what I supposed was Obstetrics. Only a small sign expressing the goodwill of the absent party. Hello, it read, in large letters.

Finally I caught sight of a woman, of the sort who doesn't go to obstetrics wards for the fun of it. Now I'm getting somewhere, I said to myself.

I hastened back to the main reception area. Flore and her brother had disappeared. I wandered around a little, as speedily as I could, then went back to Obstetrics. I pushed open the door and soon found myself in an area furnished with chairs. Flore was there, sitting with her brother. Oh, there you are, her brother said to me. We figured it out on our own, as you see.

I accepted the criticism with no ill will. If they had figured it out on their own, it was because in fact they weren't. I was with them. I would rather have been with her, but then I had no choice. A woman in a smock approached us, asked Flore for her papers, went away again. We waited. I explained to Jean, but especially to Flore, how I'd lost my way as I was searching for Emergency. I said nothing of the woman who had fainted in the basement. I didn't want to cause any alarm.

They listened attentively. Jean was observing me with a thoughtful eye, just this side of reproachful, as if seeking, somewhere deep within himself, the grounds to offer me some token of goodwill. Not so Flore, for whom attention was little more than a pose. She had other concerns.

In the following fifteen minutes, a midwife, introducing herself as such, took Flore away to be examined. Something about her inspired confidence. In normal circumstances, I would have found her charming. But the circumstances were no longer normal. I was waiting for a woman to give me a child. I was waiting, most of all, for that woman to return to me after having the child. For her to cleave in two, in short. To simplify things.

I hadn't yet been identified as the father. No one thought to ask the question. As things now stood, Jean could have assumed that role just as well as I for the purposes of the institution. The thought that he might not be Flore's brother but in fact the father of the child briefly sent a shiver down my spine. He'd told me he was only here to wait for Flore in case she was sent home. To his house, that is. What do you mean? I said. He explained that the birth might not be imminent after all. That false alarms are not unheard of. I should have known. My acquaintance with this domain was far too slight. My readings were scanty, my personal contacts few. No mothers in my circle. No families. I avoided families. No, that's not it. I knew none. Even my own, the one that included my father, my mother, and my sister, was none of my doing.

Time passed. Abnormally, Jean was quiet. I sensed something hidden there. A concern. A secret. I wanted to shake him, like that poor woman in the basement, and ask him what was wrong. I needed comfort, tranquility, careful attention. But no. Now Jean began to speak. So she finally convinced you to come, he said to me.

Excuse me? I said.

I'd heard him all too clearly. Now either I acquiesced, and I recognized, along with my paternity, my reluctance to assume it, or else I denied it, claimed to have nothing to do with it, and I had nothing to do with it. Anyway, you came, Jean repeated, and I thank you for it. I didn't answer. I was thinking of the other one, the one Flore hadn't finally managed to convince, the one she left behind in Paris. The one who let her leave. She'd met me just in time, just before the train she should have taken with someone else. Fine with me, I said to myself. I don't need much space. My big apartment isn't for me. All I need is a spot, just one little spot on this earth, just big enough to stretch out my arms. Toward that woman.

The midwife was approaching, but there's no connection.

You can come in, she told me. The labor has begun.

I knew just what that word meant, coming from her. On the other hand, I couldn't understand how she had known to speak to me. Flore must have mentioned me, described me, because no one had asked who I was. Had they asked, I would gladly have declared my identity: Gavarine, Luc. But no. A simple description had been enough to sum me up, spoken by Flore to the midwife. A portrait. Fully drawn in three little lines, no doubt. I wondered about their contents. In what Flore had said, perhaps, lay her opinion of me. The man wearing the jacket, yes, in this heat, I imagined, average size, brown eyes. With a briefcase. No, she wouldn't have said that. A satchel. Smaller than the other one. My brother, I mean.

In the meantime, Flore wanted me present beside her. Some people have career ambitions. Not me. I had only one ambition in life: a little love. Flore was offering me more than that: her hand. Her hand to hold, as she lay awaiting the child, entangled in the mass of, I imagined, unbearably intense and contradictory sensations now beginning to invade her. To rip her apart, I thought. I'm coming, I said.

To the midwife, this all seemed quite natural. I was no longer just a member of the family. I had a role to play in the workings of the hospital. The role of the father. Unless the midwife had seen through me. At the very least, let's say that I'd been entrusted with the role of the man. Quite a part. I caught my breath. I'd lost it, just like at the pool.

That was all so distant now.

I was ushered into a little room. Hooked up to a monitor, Flore lay outstretched on a rolling bed. The water's broken, she told me when she saw me. I'm not supposed to stand up. I would imagine not, I said. I'll leave you alone, the midwife said.

I walked toward Flore, trying to find the right words. Finally I asked her how it was going. Fine, she told me. You want me to stay? I said. Yes, she said. She had pale eyes, pale blue, I think. I can never remember the color of people's eyes, only the look. But she wasn't looking at me. Or at anything. I touched her hand. Thanks, she said. Oh dear, I thought. I don't want you to thank me, I said. I'm not doing you a favor. I'm helping you. Excuse me? she said. There's such an echo in here. I love you, I said.

She took my hand. In her defense, I was standing just next to her. Don't say things like that, she said. But I want to, I said. That's what you're thinking? she said. Yes, I said. She squeezed my hand. You can't love me already, she said, you've hardly seen me. A little at the pool, with my goggles on, a tiny bit more outside the pool, in the café, from far away in the train, then only in profile, and not at all in the car. But I see you, I said. I see you now. Now I love you, I lied. Now that I see you.

How do I look? she asked me.

Not beautiful, I said. That's not the word. Like my heart. The way I saw you before I met you. You're pale.

Because I'm tired.

No, I said. You're always pale. I like your paleness. And you have eyes.

Yes? Flore asked me.

88

She seemed interested. Weary too. Interested and weary.

I like your eyes, I said.

How's my conversation? she said.

Terrific, I said. I like to hear you talk.

You're talking about my voice.

Yes, I said, I'm talking about your voice.

Well, I'm talking about my conversation.

I don't really care about conversation, I explained. I'm more interested in voices. But I like your conversation too. You don't talk much.

You neither.

No, I said.

But we have to talk, she said to me. You have to talk to me. I'm afraid.

She squeezed my hand.

Just because it doesn't show, she said. I'm really afraid.

She seemed exhausted.

There's no reason to be afraid, I said.

Yes there is, she said. Oh yes there is.

I'm here, I said.

Say that again, she said.

I'm here, I said.

I think I'm going to sleep a little now, she said.

She closed her eyes. That's right, I murmured. Rest, little Flore. And I stroked her temple. No, she said. She opened her eyes. Don't call me that. And don't stroke my temple. Hold my hand.

Right, I said. OK.

She closed her eyes.

Call me what you did just now, she said to me.

And so I did. Unconvincingly.

It was better before, she said to me.

I know, I said. I lost my concentration.

89

The hell with it, she said. I'm not sleepy. Aaaah, she added.

She clutched at her stomach. It passed. Then she looked at her watch. Ten minutes, she said.

The midwife came in.

Can you leave us alone? she asked me. Five minutes.

I left them to their minutes. I looked for a chair in the hallway. I needed a rest. The midwife came for me as soon as I'd sat down.

We're going into the delivery room, she told me. If you could follow me.

I could follow her, yes. I followed. I returned to the little room. Flore wasn't there anymore. Come with me, said the midwife.

This next one was larger. Flore was sitting on the edge of the same bed, perfectly still, with a man hunched over her back. We're giving her the epidural, the midwife told me. I can see that, I said. The man detached himself from Flore's back. I'll leave you to it, he said. They went out, the two of them, and we found ourselves alone again. Flore sat facing the wall, and all I could see of her was her bare back, her shoulders holding up the hospital gown before her, her panties. Sit down somewhere, she said.

I spotted a chair, the only one gracing the room.

We have to wait a while longer, she said to me.

Do you want me to talk to you?

Yes, she said.

Do you remember what I said to you a while ago?

Yes, she said, but I'd rather not answer.

Right, I said. Then I'm going to tell you a story. It's not a pleasant story.

Oh no, she said, please!

Right, I said.

90

What's your story?

She'd turned her head.

It's the story of a man who carried a briefcase, I began. And you know what? There was nothing inside his briefcase.

That's not a story, Flore said. Besides, I think I already know it.

It may not be a story, I said, but it's my briefcase. You want to know what comes next?

Yes, she said.

The fact is, you're right; it's not a story. It's a serial. And I don't know what comes next.

You're playing games with me.

No, I said. I need you. And there's the baby on the way too. I want you to have it. I'd like you to be happy.

Me too, she said. I'd like to be happy too.

Then we were no longer alone. Still, I noted that we had been. That it was possible to be. We might be again, I said to myself, if things work out.

Soon we were five. To my left, Flore. Flore's head. At the head of the bed. Down at the foot, the anesthetist, the midwife, the obstetrician. The latter a newcomer. A proud air about him. His eye precise, his gestures confident, his speech smooth. Albeit infrequent. Comforting, all in all. Perfect. And Flore, the other side of Flore. As seen from the foot of the bed, that is. Thighs apart. Covered by the gown, fortunately, from my point of view. A domain reserved for specialists. No doubt Flore had her own sense of it, but one based more on suppositions than direct knowledge. Saw nothing. Could only feel. The child inside her, of course, and her as well around the child, and her again down there, far away, facing the end of the bed, facing the gaze of the others. Something exposed, public. Something ordinarily kept hidden. But things have changed. The boundaries. The body. The preoccupation with the body. The thoughts in the mind.

That's essentially what the look in her eyes was saying. She herself wasn't saying much. Just breathing. That's right, said the midwife. You're doing just fine. Keep calm. You're only at seven centimeters. So, I said to myself, a birth isn't simply a matter of minutes. It's a matter of centimeters too. Not centimeters per minute, no. But a question of speed, yes.

Don't push, said the midwife. Not now. Not yet. The cervix has to open wider. She clarified. I don't know what she said. A noise drowned her out. A cry. A woman, next door, crying out. At some length. I moved away from Flore. I didn't want to see her reaction. Then I came back to the head of the bed. That was my place.

It doesn't hurt, Flore told me quietly, don't worry. I'm not even afraid it will hurt. I can hardly feel a thing.

I was more than a little uncomfortable. Flore had called me *vous*, hardly the thing to call a husband, even in front of the staff.

But the staff showed little interest. On the monitor screen, the staff was observing graphs. On Flore's stomach, placing hands. Had business to conduct between her thighs as well. The staff seemed to be paying me comparatively little mind. But I felt no rancor. I was happy to go unnoticed, deep at the heart of this process. Unnoticed, soon, even by myself. I'd stopped attending to myself. I kept my eyes on what I was supposed to keep my eyes on: the look in Flore's eyes, essentially. It was changing. Not changing direction, because it was still fixed on the ceiling, so unwavering that I was afraid she might be about to faint. No. Changing brightness. I saw it darken. Then go out. Flore paled, gritted her teeth. Wait, said the midwife. She was at Flore's side now, palpating her stomach, like bread dough. Now, she said. Yes. You can start now. Push.

Flore's neck swelled. It grew wider toward the base, not so round, her two tendons, one on each side, forming a trapezoid, the skin stretched over them like a tent. Her jaws were clenched so tight I thought they might break. Her face turned blood red. Right, I said to myself. Now we're getting somewhere.

Flore was far away, of course. In that push, yes. But the push came from somewhere before the midwife's words. It was her own push, hers alone, prior to everything, words, protocols, techniques. I should say that I was pleased to see this. Rarely in my life had I felt any desire to participate. To such an extent, I mean. Now Flore was giving me that chance. There is a word, a name, whose use I customarily disdain, but which will be of use to me here: supporter. That's what I was. I was discovering encouragement. Adherence to a cause. All I needed was a slogan. I didn't know what to say. Go for it seemed too strong. Particularly because such an imperative would have implied, discreetly but perceptibly, a kind of barefaced familiarity that somehow didn't feel right in the wake of her previous formality. Although. Flore needed a good strong sentence. And so did I. Yes, I finally said. That's good. Go on.

I wasn't sure she'd really meant for me to come this far. But there I was, still at her side. I don't think she had any complaints. She'd grasped my hand. I could feel she was weak. And since – I say this in passing – she was all I had eyes for, I saw her weakness in the most general terms. Women are weak, I generalized pensively, even as I exhorted this particular woman to be strong. They find it so painfully difficult to deliver the children they want so badly. They're not made for it. It's too stupid. Men could. But they can't. That's how it is. Badly planned, badly conceived.

Because, I thought to myself, it's no good telling me about the epidural. I know all about it, thanks. I can see. Flore is in no pain, that's true. Isn't crying out, seemingly not. But she's puffing. And she surely is laboring. Overcome with exhaustion. Such a pity. She isn't even pushing anymore, that will give you an idea. She who wanted so much to push. Whose only goal was to push. She pushed, what? Twice. Nothing. When what she has to do is push again. And again. Come on, said the midwife, you have to push again. I can't do it, said Flore. Yes, you can, said the midwife. Go on, I said. Come on, the midwife said.

Flore pushed. No effort was being spared now. The staff and I could have urged her on to her death. We found words. Other words. Sometimes they intermingled. And now that strength,

94

the strength I thought had deserted Flore, now it came to her. From where I don't know. An unreal strength, improbable. But I believed in it. As in a miracle. Which is what it was. Flore pushed. I couldn't see her face now. To my eye, her face was nothing but suffering, robbed of its beauty, but she wasn't beautiful anyway, I've said that already, no, what her face was robbed of was any idea of beauty, any trace that might serve to recall beauty such as it exists in the minds of men when they imagine women – or so at least I supposed, not knowing much about men, I've heard tell of them, here and there – anyway, her face was the opposite of beauty; it was suffering. Not fatigue, not exhaustion, no. Or else exhaustion made suffering, an exhaustion that creeps up and pounces, wrings out the body like dry laundry, as if the body, drained of its strength, still had something more to lose, that weakness itself, maybe, as if an inability to do anything more had become something palpable, something else that pain could seize and bend to its will.

The same scene was repeated. The same cycle. Flore, spent, finding her strength. We couldn't go on much longer. I've forgotten how much time passed this way, how many times Flore had to begin anew, before to the midwife's lips, as dry as ours, this sentence came: I can see the head.

I looked at Flore's. She looked like nothing, like no one. Like some sort of phenomenon, maybe. From the realm of physics. That must have been what she looked like, to the extent that such a phenomenon can be made flesh. A sort of composite portrait, incarnated for the sake of tradition. Of a woman, any woman, who had given herself over to this sort of experience. Dilation. Distortion. Saturation. That's what you are now. Come on, show us how it is.

Don't relax, the midwife was chanting, go on. She was repeating herself, of course. As we all do. A sort of routine, but now gathering steam. The same gestures, the same words, suddenly erupting. The midwife, meanwhile, didn't seem particularly concerned. I was. I was wondering what they do when the child can't come through. When it stays inside. No, I later remembered. The forceps. Exist. But I didn't think of that then. I was imagining the child once the head was out, strangled by the cervix – the picture I had in my mind could hardly have been more naive, but it was a pregnant one nonetheless – the cervix, which, you see, although wide open at first, then closes down over the little neck, I was saying to myself. Naturally. It was more beautiful. More tragically beautiful. And I imagined the woman especially, Flore, fulfilled, bound up in its flesh. Not the flesh of her flesh, of course. While you're at it. It's more horrible. No, I said to myself. Don't imagine. Don't show what you're imagining. Help her.

But I couldn't do it. I was out of sweat, like everyone else in this room. Out of faith. I took Flore by the shoulders, all the same. To support her. No. To block her way. Now, I said to myself, she can't back out. Blocked at the shoulders on one side, her feet in the stirrups on the other, now she has no choice. Nor do I, come to that. It has to come through her. Her through whom it must come. It must. Yes, said the midwife. That's it. Go go go. Here we go now.

What do you mean, Now? I said to myself. What is she talking about? What does she think we've been doing all this time? Something like three hours. So Now, no, I'm not going to let her get away with a word like that. Never. Not Now. Anything you like, but not Now. Here we go, fine, that will do. Let's go, OK, but. Well, said the midwife. Yes? I said. She wasn't looking at me. She was looking at Flore. It's a girl, she said.

96

I hadn't even seen Flore relax. Hadn't seen the child. Flore was smiling. She was relaxed, finally, vaguely, and had been for a good fifteen seconds at least. And smiling. That sort of smile. Not the one I knew. Then I saw the child. In the arms of that woman. Who lay her down on top of Flore. The number of men who've seen this, I said to myself. And now me. I see it. Her. That child. Who isn't mine. Not even a little. That little girl. A little girl. Her little girl. Not her little boy. Surprise.

I tried to find something to say to Flore. Failing in this, I waited for a look. That sort of look. The sort a woman gives to the man who. But no. Nothing. Of course. Flore was looking at the child. Didn't have much of a view, actually. Found the strength again to raise her head. Felt one hand. Whereas I could see. Clearly. Which is to say not much. My dream of a child. Alive. The child, not the dream. The dream, for its part, was dying. I would never have a child. Too late. And everyone knows what a child is, at this stage. Even a little girl. The cry. The movements. The face. My God, I said to myself.

If you'd like to come this way, the midwife said to me.

Yes, I said.

You can lose hope. And still be ready. I was. I stood by, with the child, as they washed her with a sponge. Flore had let me come here, had even asked me to. Could easily not have. But had. And so here I am. And I stay. I go on. I don't back out. They held out some scissors. Toward me. Big ones. Not an obligation. An offer. I looked at Flore. She looked back, encouraging me. I see, I thought. Really. Fine, I said. Yes, I went on to say. I brought the scissors closer. Um, I said. I looked at the midwife. Then at

97

the cord, between the two blades. There, she said to me. She was pointing at the middle. You mean there? I said. Yes, she said. It's not a little far away? I said. Far away from what? she said to me. I mean a little close, I said. To the child. No, she told me, that's the middle. Look. Yes, I see, I said. Well, she said, go on. Yes, I said. And I squeezed the scissors. Nothing.

I don't know if I can do it, I said. It's hard. Yes, the midwife said, that's normal. Just give it a good squeeze. All at once? I said. All at once, she said. Yes, I said. Here, I added, do it yourself, it'll be easier that way. No, she told me, you can do it, I think you want to do it. You're right, I said. You're right. I'll try again. I tried again. Well now, said the midwife. You see. You did it. Congratulations, she said. Thanks, I said. She took the remainder of the cord, knotted it. I'm feeling a bit strange, I said. I'd been holding out the scissors toward her for ten seconds. She took them. Go sit down now, she said to me. We won't be needing you for a while.

Me neither. I didn't need myself. Just a chair. And other people. The midwife was taking samples from the child with a cotton swab. Nose, throat, ears. Now Flore was looking at me. As if to say something important that I should have understood. I didn't understand. Her gaze was full of tenderness. It got in the way. You could hardly see the love behind it. Which you supposed was there. Which you might suppose.

The midwife lifted the child from Flore's stomach. She howled. Not the midwife, no. She remained perfectly calm. You coming? she said to me, holding the child. Not a suggestion this time. I stood up, followed them to the bathtub. The size of the bathtub. Watch, the midwife said to me, I'm going to put her in. And so she did. With the palm of her hand. Holding her head. You want to hold her? she said to me. I've come this far, I said. Like this, she said. She showed me. I see, I said. And I held her

98

head. Easy enough. All you have to do is hold. Don't lift up under any circumstances. It's not a weight. Just a form there in your hands. Not hard, no. Firm. You can feel the bone beneath it. Not a particularly hard bone. Not particularly soft either. The skull is there, anyway. You're holding a head. Otherwise it will fall. It's like standing at the edge of a cliff. High above it all, including your fear. Once you stop thinking about it, there's no problem. And there was no problem. I'd stopped thinking.

Then they took her away from me. Strange sensation. They carried her off in her flannel blanket. We're going to weigh her, the midwife told me. You can stay here. Can I come? If you like. No, I said.

In the end, I wanted to stay. To look after Flore. There were still people in the delivery room. And things to do. Flore was contracting. Now, said the obstetrician. All this time he hadn't said a word. One more time. Push.

This part was easier. Faster. Fifteen minutes. Then the doctor pulled on the cord. So I supposed. It was finished. The labor was over. Still a bit early to be thinking about a vacation, but Flore relaxed. Completely. I came to her side, seeing she was alone for the moment. The staff was standing by, idly. She wondered why. I'd already asked. They have to sew you up, I said. They made an incision. We're waiting for someone.

We waited a long time. Too long. Flore was having cramps, her feet still in the stirrups. We talked about other things. So I bought a new one, I said. I'd lost the one before. That should tell you who I am. Unusual. But not so very. I'd like us to live together.

That's a beginning, she said.

I saw the problem in her sentence. The That. I didn't ask whether it stood for what I'd just said or for what we'd just done. Because we'd done something, it seemed to me. After all.

A young man entered. Unceremoniously, he settled in between Flore's thighs to sew her up. Needle, thread. He was muttering. Having difficulties. Me too: difficulty believing this was happening. Shit! he said, eventually. An intern, I supposed. I can't believe this, I said to myself. I wanted to grab him by the shoulders and give him a shake. But I was afraid to, for Flore's sake. The midwife came in, offered him some advice. Where am I? I asked myself. Where are we? What's with these people? Calm down, I told myself. There's nothing you can do about it. You should be used to that by now. So get a grip. Get hold of yourself.

You can't feel anything when they're sewing you up, of course. But Flore was coming to the end of her strength. The far end. Because it was over. Really over. Nothing more to do. It wasn't until the next day, as if finally at leisure to do so, that she began to feel the pain.

I returned to the child. I'd been summoned. Three kilos four hundred thirty grams, the midwife told me. Forty-eight centimeters. The numbers meant nothing to me. All I knew were measurements. The ones that come in threes, to describe women. And even then, not by heart. I looked at Maude. Florence, who called herself Flore, had named her Maude. The power to name. She'd taken it upon herself, serenely. I was dumbstruck.

It was the midwife who told me. I pretended to know. Maude, I said. But I wasn't talking to the child. Didn't dare. Just calling someone by name, anyone, just that, is already hard enough for me. So with her. Maude. I said her name, for myself. I murmured, to be precise.

Next, I saw her dressed. The midwife dressed her. Flore had brought a few things along. A sleepsuit, classic cut, froglike, perfect to clothe a frog, a large frog. With scallops. A little too big, maybe. Maude was lost inside it. Little frog. They made some tucks.

I gave her my index finger. She took it. A well-known thing. The little hand closing tight. The joints, at the knuckles. Undefined as yet. Rounded. The little fingers. The strength when it squeezes. The astonishment that arouses. The emotion. I'm speaking to the fathers out there. They can imagine me. I was just like them. Worse. Because I hadn't fathered this child. And she was there all the same. As if. Almost exactly as if. So nearly. Not how it was for them. Not at all. Fathers make me laugh. The way they believe in it all. Their astonishment. Then very quickly. My daughter. Whereas me. I knew.

Not the midwife. She didn't know. Looked at me as if. Although. But what matter. Watchfully. But I was relaxed. Perfectly. Much more relaxed than if. The child was really no problem. I would have taken her. Assuming Flore hadn't had her. Or had had her, rather, and was now no more. That happens sometimes. I would have taken her. Adopted her. No problem. Here, the midwife said.

She held out a bottle. A small bottle, as for a hamster. You can give it to her, she said. It's her first.

OK, OK, I thought. No problem. And indeed. I took the bottle. My cool, just then. Wait, the midwife said to me. You're holding it wrong. What? I said. The baby, she said to me. Oh, I said. No, she said, excuse me. Pardon? I said. No, she said, you're holding her right. It's me. My nerves. You're holding her very well. These births always make me nervous. I can't get used to it.

Are you all like that, in your line of work? I asked her. No, she told me. It's just me. You know, I can understand that, I said. I'd be the same. I added. Holding Maude. Naturally. The movements of a person making her way into the world. Me too. So that I could hold her. Her form, in the hollow of my arm. Curled up, yes. Her little head resting. And in the other hand, the bottle. The way you hold the bottle. Relaxed. Its accessibility. And so gluttonous. I was impressed. Myself, I nibble.

All right, that will be fine now, the midwife said to me. I have to take her away from you again. She has to have her Apgar. I understand, I said. If she has to have her Apgar. I was trying to seem casual. Nice woman, the midwife. That look. That mouth. The words she put into it. The thing she'd accomplished. They're going to move the mother into her room, she told me. If you want to go see her.

Fine with me. I could do without Maude for now. I could manage an hour. With Flore. No forgetting Flore. After all, she was the one who. And who I. A team. I loved her all the more for it. I needed her. Her as a mother. A new woman, yes. The timing was perfect. I couldn't have wished for any other mother, now. And I was only too happy to let Maude keep hers. Everything was falling into place.

I don't know if Flore suspected. That I loved her all the more. That I loved her less yesterday, then. That I'd forgotten the woman from yesterday, in fact. The pool, all that. Up to the train. Even when she was pregnant, I loved her less. I was over that. If I'd met her now, awaiting the child, I'm not sure I would have taken it, the train I mean. I was glad, cravenly, that I didn't have to tell her so. She might have taken it amiss. Assuming she remembered her.

But no. When I came into the room again, I saw at once that she'd accepted herself. That she'd drawn a line over the preceding day. That she would now slim down in short order. Organize herself around new principles. That's more like it, I said, when she saw me. Everything seems to be going well. Yes, she told me. I'm fine. But I'm afraid it's going to hurt. No, I said. Yes, she said. And that it won't go away. Not soon. I feel so frail.

She fought back a sob.

Go on, I said. Cry. If it'll make you feel better.

Stop it, she said to me. Don't tell me what to do. I'm sick of everyone telling me what to do.

I'd never known her like this. Angry. And at me too. I couldn't think of anything else to wish for. And I'd noticed the form of her verbs. Stop it. Don't tell me. With *tu*, not *vous*. What they held within them. Things are taking shape, I said to myself.

They headed us toward the room, in the elevator. What about the baby? she said to me. I want to see her.

I looked at the nurse. She was dealing with the bed, pushing it into place, pressing buttons, closing doors. Never far away. But Flore was talking to me.

I saw her, I said. You'll see her. She's very nice. Lively. She has your eyes.

My eyes?

Yes, I said. Open.

I want to see her.

Did you hear that? I said.

Speaking to the nurse.

Don't worry, she said. She'll see her.

When? said Flore.

Here, right away. Once you've settled into your room. We'll bring her in.

That seemed clear. We asked for nothing more. The room was pleasant. Private. A little noisy, from the boulevard. How did it go? Flore asked me.

What go? I said.

The delivery.

Oh, I said.

You were there, you saw it. Not me. Nothing.

Yes, I said, I understand. Fine. It went fine. Except the incision.

You see. I knew it.

No, I said, that's not what I meant. Sewing you up, I meant. That guy.

What?

He wasn't very proper. He was crude.

What about the suture?

I don't know.

It's crude, that's it, isn't it? It's a crude suture?

I don't know anything.

I knew it. I knew it was going to hurt.

No, no, I said. Well, maybe. Maybe you should tell yourself it's going to hurt. Just in case.

I was dizzy. Our *tus* were making me drunk. Out of the habit, clearly. And then suddenly finding myself strolling over the summits. The loftiest peaks, in our words. But Flore wasn't listening. She was sticking to her fears. I was beginning to wonder if she'd even noticed my person, just a little. The person I was using. The informal second. All the same, it was a beautiful exchange, to me at least. Her insouciance. At my closeness to her. As if I'd been close with her before, as if my words could never change that. Maybe because I was close. Too close. So it really didn't matter what I said. As long as I was there.

The path Flore was driving me down. Perhaps all on my own. Or let's say the leap she was forcing me to take. To which she was inspiring me, at best. Just by keeping quiet now.

The child appeared. In the arms of the midwife. Then in Flore's. No sound from the boulevard now. The room was full of the two of them. I could have bent over then. Over the one and the other. But no, best wait a while. Then attach myself to them. Photo. The man with one arm around the woman's shoulder, usually. The woman enveloping the child in her gaze and in her arms. Smiles. Silliness. I had better things to do. Wait. Wait until Flore gets tired of this. Of holding her. Obviously, that might take some time. But she was holding her wrong. Maude was howling. What's the matter with her? said Flore.

I don't know, I said. Babies cry.

There's always a reason.

I couldn't disagree.

The nurse had left us to our own devices. We rang. A neonatologist appeared. In a library, you can spot the librarians. This was a maternity ward.

She's crying, said Flore.

She cries a lot, I explained.

She won't stop, Flore added.

We could hardly hear each other. We were forced to raise our voices. To shout, even. And Maude was screaming. Nothing articulate yet, from her. But a will, already. A presence.

Maybe she's hungry, said the neonatologist.

Flore and I looked at each other, clapping hand to forehead. Then laughed.

I never would have thought of that, she said.

I added nothing. As an admission of idiocy, that seemed quite sufficient, so I kept my peace. And all the more so because now, after the child, and then the neonatologist, there now appeared Flore's breast. She'd been keeping it up her sleeve. She opted for the left. I've always wondered why. Never aloud, to her. I still don't know. I say this because I'd like to talk about that breast a little. Oh yes. That would be a great pleasure. But try to imagine the left one. That might help.

So. How to say it. We've all seen breasts. I'm speaking primarily to men here. But I'm not excluding the women. Obviously. Breasts, then. We've all seen them. And sometimes even one breast. But generally the second one isn't far behind. Appears in turn. At some point. A question of rhythm, of mood. Not this time. And you know it. You know that in this situation, or at least in this particular sequence, for there will be others, you know that too, other sequences, you know that one breast will do. Will do perfectly. So you have this breast. Period. This left breast. Which, in the present case, let us note, you've never seen before. In its entirety, that is. That's less common. What's uncommon about it, just to be sure we understand each other, is that this isn't happening in a park, a public park. A mother on a bench. And you pass by. Or read the newspaper. On that same bench. You raise an eyelid. No. You're not reading the newspaper. You've met this woman in a swimming pool because of a telephone call. A telephone call from another woman. Following upon a silence. From yet another woman, yes. And, one thing leading to another, here you are. Alone with this woman. Suddenly. You've sat in on her delivery, you've helped her through it, through the delivery, you even call her *tu* now – in short, for the past twenty-four hours you've been taking giant steps toward this woman, but all the same you scarcely know her. Her sex, more or less. And even there. From three quarters, at best. In conditions that could hardly be called ideal. Surely not. But not her breast, no. Not the breast that now comes into view. And right or left, in the end, it matters little. It's a large breast. No. Grown large. Small in the beginning, perhaps, but that's of no account. Even the areola: you can try to describe it, its form, its color, rich in both cases, but you're still only skimming the surface of the question, not facing it head on. Without the nipple, you don't have it. We all remember the cylinder from our study of geometry. It's a recognized shape. Now imagine that cylinder, for lack of anything better, made of lightweight felt. Cut it short. For a cylinder, as geometry commonly represents it, is always too long. What interests you in this case is a short cylinder. Relatively. Now consider the base. Broaden it. Tamp it all down. Not too much. A certain stiffness is essential. Or rather a kind of springiness. And still. Yes? Well, even now, it's still no good. You've forgotten the breast itself.

Besides, you've only had one short glance at it. There's still more to see. Although a short glance becomes a long one, when faced with this breast. But in any case, you have this breast. Full. Atypically firm. But things are happening. The child can't find the nipple. Hard to figure. How, you wonder, could it not find the nipple? How can that be? If I, you briefly think. Because your ignorance has led you into error. You don't realize, at first, that the child doesn't see the nipple. Her eyes are open, but she doesn't see it. Whereas for you, of course, it's the opposite. You see it. But you close your eyes. Not simply politeness. A reflex. To keep from seeing that. That nipple. The mother hasn't aimed the child properly. And she's holding it wrong too. And don't think it's easy. Or innate. It's not innate. It's exhausting. The woman can't go on. Has no strength left to devote to that movement, or rather that complex of movements. Proffer the breast, maintain the child. Can't quite master the intricacies. The child cries. Discomfiture. And when you're me, in such a situation, you don't just stand by doing nothing. You react. You help.

Wait, I said.

And I stood up.

I was sitting down.

You want to do it? said the neonatologist.

I'd forgotten her. She was there. Ready to advise. To intervene.

Thanks, I said.

And I placed myself behind Flore. Sitting on the bed, I supported her with one arm, then undertook to coordinate the aforementioned two movements. United them. I closed the gap. Little Maude and Flore's breast. Her big breast. I made them one.

You're not always going to be around, the neonatologist intervened. There's a technique. May I?

Next time, said Flore. It'll be fine for now.

As you like, said the neonatologist.

She was smiling, took it well. Me too. I didn't know what to think anymore. Too much love, I said to myself. The happiness here. Settling in. Say, it says to itself, not a bad thing, this. These people. Supposing I stuck around for a while.

We stayed alone, just the three of us. Fully intending to survive, Maude had a plan. To drink a lot. For a long time. Flore looked at her watch again. Me too. Between my eye and her watch, the curve of her breast. Maude's little face, clinging to it. And that feeling. The feeling that. Yes, like a while ago. Just now. No. I wouldn't have sworn to it. That Flore felt. The same thing, yes. As I was feeling. Not a feeling, no. A certainty. Yes. Just a feeling.

We spent several hours with Maude this way, and soon evening was coming on. Sometimes Maude slept; sometimes she awoke, crying, and we had to feed her. When she slept, we talked about her. When she nursed, we talked to her. Especially Flore. It was difficult for me to talk to the child in front of her. I didn't know what the latter saw me as representing, with respect to the former. Obviously not a father. My greatest fear was that some idle word, carelessly let slip, might arouse in Flore's mind the idea of a counterfeit avuncular title as the thing for me. That would have been horrible.

Nevertheless, I was happy to stay in the background, noting that, as she spoke to Maude, calling her by name, nickname, adjective, but also touching her, embracing her, exerting various pressures on her, conjugating various actions in various moods and, from my point of view, then, various verbs, active, passive, reflexive, even unreflecting sometimes, or pensive, Flore did not entirely neglect my presence. A glance was cast my way from time to time, in search of acquiescence or elaboration, a sentence occasionally submitted to me in cadences that invited repetition. And so I elaborated, I repeated, I even innovated, spotlighting some secondary characteristic of the child, some slight but persistent behavior that Flore, overburdened by the task of attention, overcome with love, had not had the opportunity to grasp. Then she turned back toward the child and for many long moments had eyes only for her, even when she couldn't touch her, lying there in the little bed, next to her own but behind a glass panel, where the neonatologist insisted she reside between nursings so as to give her mother a rest. The same neonatologist then proceeded, elevating the child's two legs with one hand – although legs, here, seems to me too strong a word, or too long, to designate what first appeared uncertainly to me only as an assemblage of thighs, feet, and calves, vaguely linked by articulations that half masked what they were meant to join together, the whole thing melding into a single pink, bulging, pudgy vision – the same neonatologist, then, proceeded to address the issue of Maude's toilet and then the replacement of her diaper, each of these operations involving a finesse that would require a period of apprenticeship on Flore's part, necessarily deferred until she'd regained her strength. For weary Flore often drifted off for hours at a stretch, leaving me alone with Maude, circling her as she lay in her little bed, not daring to pick her up when she was sleeping as well, picking her up when she awoke and entrusting her to Flore, contracting the beginnings of a habit by way of this cohabitation. I'd told myself, on meeting Flore, a woman amply figured by a child, even then, a woman in whom both a child and, more hypothetically, my relation with her mother were figured, I'd told myself that should these many diffuse virtualities come to life together, it would surely give me a good shaking up. And so it had. Moved by the birth I had been, and still was. But differently. I felt – in that room where those two beings, so close but also so new to my life, generally slept – I felt at home. Whatever my role was to be, I was at home in this room, but also in the skin, not so new in the end, that I was undertaking to don. Not so new, I say, because, having this child and this woman so near me, what I felt above all was a sensation of remembering. So I continued. I pursued my existence with them. Had I met them years before, notwithstanding Maude's age, which would have varied accordingly, along with our words and gestures, I sensed that nothing would have been different. I was a part of this child, to cut a long story short, and, whatever her mother might think, I had long since been the father, and long since the mother had been my wife. I'd been waiting for them, and now they were here. Nothing could be more ordinary. I'd forgotten everything else. I was at home.

Except for one detail. I didn't know where I'd be sleeping. The room had been laid out with no bed for me. Flore and I had never broached the subject of my couch, which, given the attentions Maude required, had scarcely had time to raise its head. Even now it only drifted over the surface of my consciousness. It was, of course, in part the tendency of the room's inhabitants – me excluded – to spend long periods asleep that had fostered this new awareness, further reinforced by my own vague sensation of fatigue. But more than that, the repeated gestures, attitudes, words, the same thought all day long, had instilled in me a sort of satiety, leaving me open, at present, to a more concrete consideration of what was to follow. A small anxiety, to be sure, not an all-consuming one. But developing all the same. I didn't dare mention it to Flore, not wishing to burden her with details. Although. Was this truly a detail? Indeed, it soon occurred to me that Flore's silence on this point might not be a silence at all. Dismissing the possibility that the interest she was capable of granting me might turn out to be nil, I concluded that to her this was simply not a problem. I would sleep somewhere. The next day, I would come and see her again. In other words, I wouldn't be taking the train back to Paris tonight. In short, I would be staying on. How, where, that I didn't know. She herself seemed entirely unpreoccupied by the question. And, not having broached the subject with her on my own behalf, I said to myself, this is where, for a number of reasons, her brother should intercede.

Indeed, he was due for a reappearance, which would be a

first step in the process. For a number of reasons, again. The first was simple, no doubt, scarcely fraught with implications but sufficiently so to deserve some mention: Jean had vanished before the delivery, ceding me his place. As a brother, it was now time he came back. With a father, if need be, a wife, children, a mother, hers, other brothers or sisters, friends. A bouquet of flowers. Say, I said to myself, I should have thought of that myself. I'm joking. I hadn't had time. And what I did went far beyond that. Far beyond any bouquet of flowers ever given to a new mother. Far beyond any bouquet of flowers at all, for that matter. I've done my bit already, thanks.

So, Jean. The brother. I said to myself. Should come back. At some point, difficult to specify perhaps but determined on the basis of an average duration. The duration of a delivery, of course. But that was variable. And it was difficult to imagine Jean, far from the hospital, counting out the hours, alone. Estimating the requisite lapse of time, as best he can, then concluding that the moment had come. By now, the child has been born. Must have been born. Or telephoning to check. No? Not yet? I'll call back.

That seemed improbable for some reason. Their fraternal bond, maybe. Its exceptional nature. No matter. The second reason why Jean should come back was me. He was obligated to carry on, I thought, with the task of welcoming me. I was new here. With nowhere to go. I was arriving at the home of a brother. I had the right to expect some sort of follow-up.

It came. At about six o'clock. A little early for dinner, of course. But I hadn't had any lunch. Flore's tray, the meager contents of Flore's tray, had dissuaded me. Besides, neither of us was hungry. But all the same. The time for a break was near. It was incarnated in the form of Jean. He entered, at ease. Having heard the news. Ah, he said. The baby. Let's have a look.

He stepped forward. Congratulated me as he passed by. Brought his index finger toward Maude's throat. Hello, Maude, he whispered. And then the index finger. Between the child's little folds, under her double chin. I knew that move; I'd made it myself. I'm Jean, he said, shaking something. From various characteristics, the way it lay in his hand, the herniated extremity, the sonorous clinking of captive particles, I realized it was a rattle. I'd never seen one so close up. Nor had Maude. She seized it, immediately let it drop as one would some impossibly heavy burden. It fell. Jean embraced his sister. So, everything went smoothly?

Luckily, the two women were awakening. Ready for anything, the pair of them. Flore said yes, not too bad. Maude cried. Then Flore. Come on now, he said. I was a little miffed at Flore. She'd been holding out. But soon I realized that Jean had nothing to do with it. Or not much. A cumulative effect, at best. His bulk saturated the space. His presence was irrefutable, like a proof. Brought the child to life. Again.

It's nothing, said Flore.

She'd taken Maude from him, this time without my help. I stood at the ready. At the end of the bed. Sitting. Jean, for his part, ignored the single chair. Just passing through, it seemed. God knows I did not find his presence indispensable at that precise moment, but I wanted him to stay. And tell me what would happen next. If my life were only a story, a story in a book, Jean would surely choose to keep me here. That's what I was telling myself. That, as an author, he would let me develop a bit. In short, I was waiting for him to better define my role. I needed to know.

You look beat, my friend, he said to me.

Me? I said.

Yes, he said. I'm going to take you home.

114

I looked at Flore. She silently acquiesced. Yes, she intimated. You've done enough. You've earned the right to go home. I couldn't disagree. But where that was to be, I still didn't know. Nor if anything more was expected of me. And still I didn't dare ask. Neither the one nor the other. I was still afraid. Such a shame, I said to myself. When you've already changed your life. When you're already somewhere else. You're still afraid. Confident but anxious, that's you. Everything's fine where you're concerned. Just fine, you might even say. Never better. But the others. That's what frightens you. You never know what they might do. And the less you know them, the more they can do. Take Jean, for instance. You don't know the first thing about him. A host of details, yes. He likes to talk. Whereas he knows everything there is to know. Everything essential. As does Flore. They haven't even had to talk it over. They know things, just like that. They sense them. Proof of their existence. Somewhere, the truth of my life exists. In their heads.

Thanks, yes, I said.

I took a step toward Flore. Unsteadily. Fainting seemed one possible solution. I made ready to collapse and lose consciousness. I remembered the woman in the basement. Standing there, then briefly tottering, then nothing. Darkness. Comfort.

At the last moment, Flore caught me with her gaze. I saw a gleam.

See you tomorrow, I said.

Rarely had I said so much to a woman in such circumstances. But it still wasn't enough. I had to make some sort of gesture. In front of Jean. I didn't particularly want to kiss Flore. Not like that. I repressed my desire, my other desire, to kiss her not like that but like this, intimately, and gave in, sick at heart, to the obligation I'd been handed. To kiss Flore like that, in front of Jean. I leaned over her. Kissed her like that. A little more. On the corner of her mouth. She put her hand on the nape of my neck. Kissed me. Like this. In front of Jean. I was about to extract myself. Not taking advantage of the moment as I should. She held me back. Gave me her tongue. I was bent double. I had to sit down. To keep from crushing her. And little Maude along with her. She was there too. We don't want to do that, I said to myself. Let's just enjoy this for two seconds. Three. Four. Um, said Jean.

I'm coming, I said.

Wait, said Flore. The list. I've checked off what I need.

She held out a piece of paper. Given to her by the neonatologist, I suppose. I'd missed that part.

Girl's diapers (pink), I read. Wipes. Eosin.

So, said Jean.

I'm coming, I said.

I hurried to collect my things. I would have followed him to the ends of the earth.

I asked him no questions until the car. Then nothing again in the car. Then still nothing. Having, in light of Flore's conduct, ruled out the possibility that he was returning me to the train station, I now feared that he would drop me at some nearby hotel. The terror, dispelled by Flore, that I would be thanked for my services and sent on my way, now that my work was done, gave way to a terror of finding myself on the sidelines. I would have a place, yes, but far away, far from the hospital, far from their lives.

But no. We drove out of the city. Here the hotels appeared only as billboards punctuating the roadside, their referents cast far afield. If such had been our destination, we would have turned left eight hundred meters ahead, or right one hundred meters after the light. And Jean wasn't turning. Only the road was turning, sinuous, beribonning the hills. A wooded region, I noted. Rock-strewn. Meanwhile, Jean once again strayed from his established image. He was a taciturn man that evening, pensive, as if obeying some protocol in which silence was the rule. I couldn't imagine what he was trying to protect. No pain emanated visibly from me, I supposed. No secret deep within me that he might have resolved to shield with his silence, lest some pointed word unintentionally puncture its fabric. Unless he was keeping a secret of his own, as I'd suspected at the hospital. Or harboring one. Did he have a wife, did he have children? There was room for doubt. I imagined myself in his place. He had come alone to pick up Flore at the station, and he'd come back alone to see her. I like this part of the country, he said to me (his gaze skewered the landscape as it skimmed past the window). Not really that far south, but already turning dry. More yellow than green. This is all a big limestone plateau.

Finally. My guide had begun to guide me. I found his commentary soothing. We climbed a hillside, then dove again. Continued alongside a superhighway. Recent, by the look of it. It made us seem slow. A road was foretold, intersecting with this one. At the crossroads an old man stood near a shelter, waiting for a bus. On the left, a billboard announced the existence of caverns.

We took the intersecting road. It climbed, briefly, narrow, then contracted farther as it entered a stand of oaks. We trundled through a cheery little woods. I call it cheery because it was sunlit. Still bright, the late afternoon light found its way through the branches here and there. I haven't yet mentioned the sun. It lit that perfect afternoon, and kept it from cooling. I felt better. As good as I had leaving Flore's arms. The environment seconded me.

Soon, we reached a still brighter spot. More oak trees, a few hornbeams, some linden, but less. Petering out, the road subdivided into paths, which in turn broadened into open areas. Compacted earth mingled with dry, broken leaves. Despite the thinning, the trees maintained a gentle shade that did not exclude an occasional intrusion of light. Never quite even, the ground formed slopes here and flat spots there. Jean parked. Farther on, the trees grew denser again. As we pulled in, I'd caught a brief glimpse, half-obstructed by trees, of three or four little buildings in a sort of semiclearing, tile-roofed, built of stone. And also another, of wood this time, atop an embankment, entered by a flight of steps. The front was papered with posters evoking wines and wine producers. Kanterbrau Beer, I read on the pediment. Bar of the Caverns.

Jean conveyed me in that direction. Sit down here, he said to me. He left me on the terrace, on a red chair beneath a yellow parasol. Coca-Cola, it said around the edge. I cast an unbelieving eye around me, but all around me lay a woods. Stretching off into the distance. Only one other car in the clearing. So there was this café. In the middle of a woods. An old café, built of wood. Near some caverns. The light danced over it all. I don't know where I am, I told myself. But I like it here.

I could see Jean from the terrace, busying himself behind the bar, which was made of logs. In a yellow room with green chairs. I had no sense of the establishment's equipment, but I guessed that no percolator was in use back there. Jean returned to the terrace carrying a tray, atop which two glasses overflowed slightly with what my host had visibly drawn from the contents of two bottles, also present, as if watching over them, the glasses that is, standing ready to top them up again as required. Wine, sweetened with a drop of liqueur. Let's have a toast, said Jean, once he'd extended a glass toward me, after he'd pulled a chair toward himself. His gaze swept over the clearing. Well, here we are, he said. This is home.

I would gladly have heard him go on to say that we were home now, to convince me that that was indeed where I was. Or even that I should make myself at home. I would have appreciated a gesture of that sort. Nevertheless, I couldn't complain of Jean's hospitality. We drank, and as we drank, I learned that these lands had been left to him by an ancestor. Who lived off the wood. But then one day. Jean pointed an index finger toward a tree hung with a hand-lettered sign. To the caverns, I read. It was an arrow, as it happened. Pointing left. It was nice to be shown arrows that evening. At the hospital I'd found one on my own and ended up lost. But then one day, Jean said again. They found that. They climbed down inside on ropes. Everything underground belongs to me, he explained, and I'm legally entitled to exploit it. That's the law. So that's how I make my living. From what's down there, underground, he repeated.

Under the effect of that word, which clearly gave him pleasure, his lips stretched laterally. Jean smiled, as if he were speaking of some seam of precious ore. Oh, he said, it's a lot of work, a lot of seeing to. It doesn't bring in much. Still, enough. In any case, more than the wood ever could have. Well, he said.

Another smile. Stretching out his arms this time. His Well was not only vague. It seemed vast. Enveloping me. Along with everything underground, no doubt. I was another precious resource. But I felt no fear of being exploited. Jean poured me another drink. Distractedly, I'd drained mine.

Yes, I said. Not only an acquiescence. A commentary too. I don't hold my liquor well. Drunkenness was driving me to ellipsis. Now we'll have a bite to eat, Jean said.

We ate on the terrace. The meal, cursory, was derived from cans and sprouted potatoes. There was no lack of wine. You going to stay here? Jean asked me.

I started. I was somewhere else entirely. How's that? I asked myself. What's happening? What's he talking about?

Then I understood. From the look on his face. Jean was asking me, simply, if I was planning to stay here. It was a question. Neutral. Descending ever so slightly, to be sure. Falling, almost insensibly, toward an affirmation, which, in turn, contained the germ of a question. What Jean was asking me, deep down, was whether it was definite. That I would stay. To be sure. Just to be sure. With an intimation, though, that he was far from opposed to the idea. But wasn't trying to push me into it. Into staying. That I was free, in other words. Free but welcome. I could just as well stay somewhere else. With Flore and the child. Decide. Not easy. In terms of choice, I'd rarely found myself commanding such capital.

I don't know, I finally said. I'm going to take some time and think about it.

Through my drunkenness, a little later, I thought I saw a young woman. Almost a girl. She appeared at the threshold of the bar. Hello, she called out to me. OK, I'm off, she breathed to Jean. Irrefutably, she was pretty, alive, existed. She was a real girl. That's the waitress, Jean told me. She was cleaning up in back. She's going home now.

She headed toward the second vehicle parked in the clearing. Started up. Drove off. We were alone, differently. More so. Faced with her departure.

Our exchanges were now reduced to single words. We lacked the strength for sentences. Or only short ones. It's peaceful, I said. Jean filled in with adverbs. Yes, he said. Remarkably. The birds were growing loquacious. We didn't interrupt. Between two trills, Jean whispered a name. Nuthatch. Bunting. The clearing was turning red. I'll show you your room, he said.

It was a long and leisurely conclusion. We progressed to the bar. Beyond, the place was divided into two parts. One behind the bar: kitchen, laundry. One at the far end of the dining room: the bedrooms, three of them. Walls marked them off. Doors were scattered here and there. Jean opened one. The low building that housed the café was expansive enough to let this room stay on the ground floor. It looked onto a butte. Here the woods rose up, looming over the clearing. The bed was large, double. I didn't know who usually slept in it. Nevertheless, the decoration betrayed a certain taste. Colors harmonized, and shapes. On a table, boxes. Cases. Apparently Jean wasn't married. I slept in Flore's bed.

Soundly. Late. Jean woke me up. The night before, he'd promised to show me the rest. The most important part, according to him. The little buildings scattered around the bar. The caverns. We ate breakfast on the terrace. Right, he said, we have plenty of time. They won't be here for an hour.

I assumed he was referring to visitors. Jean led me to the office, housed in a building not far from the caverns. Along the way I noticed a grillwork fence with a metal gate, closed, between two pillars topped by a little tile roof. Behind it lay a dim emptiness, ringed with mossy walls of stone, blanketed with leaves. A green vision. Quite unlike the bare walls in the office. Jean opened the door, invited me in, showed me a table with photograph-filled folders, a metal box. An armchair was adjoined to it. That's where I sit, he said.

My gaze lingered on the walls, in the company of the numerous posters that covered them. All around, right up to the ceiling, everything was caves, grottoes, caverns, captured with expensive cameras in spotlit darkness. An entire country, France, I realized, lay exposed and outstretched here, dragged up from below ground by flashbulbs. A land of damp stone, randomly fashioned into something vaguely Gothic. In short, I thought, the competition. Jean did not consider his cavern an island.

He sold little souvenirs as well. Necklaces, rings. By which the stone, mounted and set, perpetuated the memory of itself. It came packaged in little bags as well. Meanwhile, the iconography of the postcard racks ignored the present surroundings, widened the horizons, showed the sky, the hills, even overflowed the region, spilled southward, invited the viewer on a journey. The caverns' clientele was a transitory one. This was freely acknowledged. What they were offered here was only a point of departure for their travels. Or a goal. Much the same thing in either case. Whereas I, of course. This was a confirmation. I was here. No sense going farther.

122

The girl isn't here yet, Jean observed. The guide. He pointed toward a kitchen clock between two grottoes. It overlapped onto the posters. No room. We open at ten o'clock, he said.

Five till, the clock said.

The sound of an engine now made itself heard. Jean cursed. We went outside. It was a bus. A small bus, twelve people. They emerged. A man strode toward us. He was the guide. Not the girl guide. These people's guide. Hello, said Jean. We're about to open. You're not late.

He left them standing in the clearing. We came back to the office. Jean sat down at the table, and the guide entered. The office door hadn't shut. Without further delay, Jean opened the box, tore off the tickets, sold them. Just another couple of minutes, he said to the guide. We're waiting for the guide. Before this guide, I don't know why, he no longer dared call her the girl. She'll be along, he went on, giving himself away. She should be here soon.

She wasn't. Ensconced before a display rack, I studied the postcards. I don't like people in difficulty. I would gladly have helped him if I could. Right, said Jean to the guide, let's go. If you could just give me one more second.

He left his chair, came toward me, pulled me aside, over by the necklaces. Luc, he said to me. I need you. The night before, spurred on by drink, the familiar *tu* had wormed its way, unobstructed, into our conversation. Without really cultivating it, we let it grow.

Can you watch the cashbox? he asked me. I'm going to show them around myself. The ticket prices are written on the table. If the guide comes, you can explain. Explain what? I said. I don't know, he said. Who you are. Me? I said. Yes, he said. Of course. And you can tell them. About the delay.

How do you mean?

No, he said. Nothing. I'll see to that later.

He left me alone behind the table. Through a window I saw the guide rounding up his group, then Jean taking over to guide them toward the caverns. Then it was through the open door that I saw Jean open the gate to the caverns. They all went underground together. I unfolded a folder.

I couldn't concentrate. I jumped from one photo to the next. I drummed my fingers on the tabletop, picked up the phone, hung it up again. Say, I said to myself, a telephone. I hadn't noticed it before. But I didn't have the number of the hospital. So I couldn't call Flore. But I wanted to call Flore. Now. Because of the telephone. Otherwise I would have just thought about it. So I thought about it. All the more. I knew that visitors were not permitted at the hospital in the morning. All the same, I said to myself, we could talk.

I grew impatient. Afternoon, I said to myself, begins at one o'clock. I'm comfortable enough here, but. I looked at the clock. Ten fifteen. And Jean will be back. I don't even know when. He never said how long the tour lasts. He'll come back up, and then what? Will I even be able to tell him? That I miss Flore, yes. His sister. Is he capable of understanding that?

He must be, I said to myself. He is. I can see he is. He's proven it. I'll wait for him to come up. And then I'll tell him. I miss Flore. Do you have the number of the hospital? Give it to me, would you? I need to know how Maude is doing too. I know, I didn't write down the number. But you. Her brother. No? You're right, I should have written it down. But you must have it somewhere. All this time. All this time you've lived here, both of you. All this time that Flore. You must have the number around here somewhere. Surely, I said to myself. Surely he has the number. I just have to wait for him to come up again.

Except, I said to myself. Even if he does have the number.

How do I get to V—— this afternoon? Does he go with me? And if not? There is the bus stop, of course. A little far away by foot, though. He'll have to drive me. But after all. After all, he'll be going to the hospital himself. He'll drive me. She is his sister, after all. He'll be wanting to see her. His niece. He'll come with me. It's only natural. Assuming the guide girl comes, that is. And even then. How will she manage, all alone, with the caverns and the ticket desk to deal with? So Jean won't come with me, I said to myself. Or else. He's got something planned. A solution. A friend. A neighbor. I can't imagine him not having a solution. So he will come with me. I don't know how, but he'll come. I'd gladly go without him, of course. I like him, that's not the question. But, well, if I had a car. Supposing. And if I knew how to drive. If I could go to the hospital alone, just once. To see whether, without him.

That was my doubt now. I wondered if deep down. This Jean. The brother, yes. His role. In my life. His place. The place he was assuming, at least. Not to mention the place he seemed to be giving me. I'd chosen to stay, of course. Obviously. That's not what I mean.

I didn't hear the second car pull up. I only noticed it when I saw the young woman. Seeing her, then, seeing her face, I heard her car. Strange, the sound of an engine turning off, in the eyes of a woman. She waved through the office window as she passed by. And she wasn't really a woman; she was the girl from the day before. The real one. She headed straight for the bar.

The guide, for her part, did not appear. A third vehicle, then a fourth came to rest in the clearing. People entered. Hello, I said. French, like the others. I couldn't quite picture myself as a linguist.

I sold tickets. Made change. There'll be a few moments' wait, I said. We're short on staff just now. The guide will be along soon. I was alluding to Jean, in my head. I didn't know any other guides.

Forty-five minutes. That was the length of the tour. Jean reappeared. Ladies and gentlemen, he said. If you'd just follow me.

He was out of breath. The caverns must have been very deep. He went down in again. Didn't even take the time to give me a nod. I stayed at my post. In his absence, I consulted a brochure. Twenty-five meters. And no elevator, I supposed. Only to be expected, in caverns as modest as these. Small, humble, not even world-famous. But soon I was forced to abandon my reading. The visitors from the previous tour wanted souvenirs. Labeled, thankfully. I handled the sales. They left. Not to be replaced. No engine shutting off in the clearing now. Thirty minutes later (and not forty-five this time, I noted), Jean came to the surface again. Exhausted. I took on his group for souvenir purposes. There was a chair in the office, in addition to the armchair, and there he sat, leaving me to it. He was grateful. Me too. His gratitude. Then we were alone. Time for lunch, he said, don't you think?

I did. We had lunch. The waitress served us. Happily, there was no one parked in the clearing and so no customers in the bar. They served no meals there in any case. Except for staff. Which is what we were, and in the first ranks. With just a touch of pride, perhaps. But Jean was showing symptoms of anxiousness. He was thinking of his guide girl. She really should have called, he observed.

He called her, after the coffee. Ill, he told me. Very ill. That was her mother I. Well, great. A girl working toward a degree in tourism. Good at it too. She couldn't call, of course. In her condition.

It'll work out, I said.

126

Yes, Jean said to me. Of course it'll work out. It has to work out. I don't have any other choice.

I raised my eyes to the sky, of which I could see patches. I was thinking, said Jean.

I know, I said. Me too.

You wouldn't mind? he said.

I didn't do too badly this morning at the ticket desk.

Oh, said Jean, you're a lifesaver.

The one problem is this afternoon, I said.

Yes, said Jean, I understand. I understand. You want to go.

In any case, I said. I'm going to go.

I understand, said Jean. I'll manage. I have an uncle.

Well, there we are, I said. That's it. An uncle.

I'll have to get in touch with him, said Jean.

I glanced toward the telephone on the bar. There were two at the caverns. Jean had just used this one to call the guide. Now he used it again. At my insistence, perhaps. Nobody home, he said.

You can call back, I said.

Yes, he said. Obviously. And for this afternoon I'll lend you my car.

Thanks, I said. That's very kind of you. But.

You don't know how to drive.

Is it that obvious?

It seems like a safe bet.

The problem, I said, is going to be your coming with me. That's what you're about to tell me.

We can read each other like a book, he said.

Yes, I said.

I'm not going with you, he told me. I can't. Even if my uncle. We're stretched too thin here as it is. And I can't close. I don't want to close. I never close. That would be a disaster. I'll teach you to drive.

Truth be told, I had done some driving, by mistake, in my youth, in the company of a nervous instructor with no great gift for putting me at ease. And, once, I attempted the driving test for the license, alongside an underhanded examiner who allowed me to stop in fourth gear well past a red light. Who did nothing to encourage me to continue. But most of all, I'd given it up because the woman I then loved had left me after the seventh lesson, and I couldn't really see the point of learning to drive. There was no one to take anywhere.

The first of my new lessons was a brief one. I stalled in front of a group of visitors. Five of them, no more. Clambering out of their four-by-four. Requiring Jean's attentions. Then we took advantage of a lull. It was now two in the afternoon. I was impatient to see Flore. I threw the car into first gear. Bounded forward. Stalled. Jean showed me how to work my feet. The rhythm. In swimming, he said, there's the crawl. Yes, I said. I didn't want to try his patience. Here, he said, it's not the legs. It's the feet. Which move that same way. He showed me his hands. This kind of motion, he said. Alternating like this. Continuously. The feet never united. Never together. The opposite of the breaststroke.

I know all that, I said. I just have to find a way to do it.

I shifted into first gear. Didn't stall. Now I was motivated. Now second, Jean said to me. You have to shift into second. After that it's easy. First is the hardest. You're not moving. Well now, you see? he said. You're moving. Look.

I see, I said. We were turning circles in the clearing. Just the place for it. No one in front of us. If a car comes along, said Jean,

it's simple, just step on the brake. And they'll be customers anyway. You'll have things to do with them.

I was relearning fast. For third gear, we went as far as the
edge of the woods. For fourth, we drove alongside the highway.
You don't have to take that to go to V——, Jean told me. Stay
on this one. There are curves, of course. And it goes downhill.
Use the engine brake. What about parking? I said. Don't park at
the hospital, he told me. Just stop. It's summertime.

We still had to wait for the uncle. Jean had finally reached
him. He appeared at around three in the afternoon. He was an
old uncle, desiccated, from a nearby village, with a keen interest in municipal affairs. He elaborated. I understand, I said.

I left them there. Started off. Twenty meters farther on, I
heard a shout. Before I'd reached the edge of the clearing. Rearview mirror! I heard. I looked in the rearview mirror. Jean
hadn't told me about that. I could see him gesticulating, still
shouting. Rearview mirror! most likely. I couldn't hear him
anymore. I'd put some distance between us.

Then I couldn't see him anymore. I was out on the road.
Alone. At the wheel, at least. There was traffic. Not too much,
but all the same. I kept right. Braked on the hill. I was terrified
of stalling. Of finding myself idling again. Let's have none of
that, I said to myself. People passed me. I paid no mind. In front
of you, Jean had told me. Look in front of you. Hence his forgetting about the rearview mirror, of course. Nevertheless, I
briefly glanced at the sides of the road. Bordered with open
trenches. Danger. No need to tell me. I kept well away, horns
blasting long and loud around me. I was afraid. That was a new
sensation. I wasn't sure I'd ever been afraid before. In pain, yes,
but afraid, not particularly. Or maybe a distant fear, faint.

Once in the city, I realized that Jean had told me nothing of
the traffic laws. Of their relationship with the practice of driv-

129

ing. I struggled to apply the one to the other, clumsily as always. Sometimes I read, sometimes I drove. A kind of wisdom, in short, but a bit outdated. A bit too Zen. Stoplights were a particular problem. I knew the rules, but I didn't see them. Couldn't foresee them. Ran them. Or slammed on the brakes and stalled. The hardest part was finding a pharmacy for Flore's list. Beyond the stoplights, before them, I searched for green crosses. One of the latter blinked into view as one of the former turned red. That one I saw. I double-parked, made my purchases, drove off again without a hitch. I was making progress. I felt fine. Amazingly fine. Surprised. Pensive. Talented, even. I found my way to the hospital with ease. There were arrows to point the way. The logo caught your eye at once. In the parking lot, I stopped, as Jean had advised. Straddling a line of paint, but far from the wall. A little too far. My backside protruded. I couldn't see the point of exposing myself to the risks involved in starting up again, just to move forward one meter. I pulled the emergency brake. Got out of the car, judged my handiwork acceptable. A car would get by. Could, I mean. Maybe not a big one. What I couldn't picture was the volume of an ambulance. A big ambulance.

The usual litany of corridors, fire doors, unoccupied offices, and then I was with Flore again. She looked pale. She was. More than usual.

It hurts, she told me.

She'd expected as much. But that's no help. I realized I was embracing her. Her kiss reminded me. Too brief. I was bothering her. Probably not a good time. But I couldn't see why it should be forbidden to embrace a woman in pain. On the contrary. Especially on having just been reunited with her. That was what I was trying to acknowledge. I looked for a word to supplant my gesture. Just when I'd found it, she bade me to keep quiet. Her hand on my lips. It was better this way.

How's Maude? I said.

No sweeter word could have survived her censorship. Or mine. There was still a certain lack of words between us, it seemed. Nouns particularly. We had a number of verbs, it's true. A few sentences connected us, told our story. But nouns, nouns proper to us alone, of that there were none. Apart from our own names. And even there. We almost never used them with each other. But there remained Maude's name, yes.

She wasn't there. Flore explained. In every hospital's maternity wing there is a nursery. Which undertakes to care for the child when the mother so wishes. When she's tired. Or in pain. As I am, she reminded me.

How is she? I inquired.

Very well.

But not you, I said.

No, she said. Not me.

I nodded. Tried to find a rejoinder, some way forward. I had helped this woman, no one could deny it. Even in her pain, the particular pain that comes with the ultimate exertion. But I couldn't find my way into the pain that racked her now. That damn intern, I said to myself. Who sewed her up, best not to see how. But I didn't dare. No. I didn't know how to enter into that pain. Too passive, was the problem. Into her will, fine. I'd squeezed myself inside, yes. Whereas now. She wasn't fighting. She simply suffered. Simply was. And was only herself. I barely knew her.

Well, I said to myself. The main problem is words. The words I lack. Which she's forbidden me, which I've forbidden myself, in hopes of helping her. The same words we forbade ourselves just now. Especially her. For my part, it's true, I couldn't deny. I felt them, furthermore. They were coming to me. My love. I choked them back. My own. But no. Something missing. A history. No. A strength. A strength I lack, a strength she isn't giving me. Poor us, I said to myself.

Can I see her? I asked.

Obviously, she told me.

She was grimacing. Expressing her pain. Again. I touched her, all the same. Again those hands, that contact of the hands. A touch was the best I could do, now, with her. It wasn't too difficult. Touching a woman like that, because you've decided you love her, and in order for you to love her, all she has to do is want you to. And she did want that. Was willing. Wanted nothing more. But yesterday, I said. As I was leaving. What? she said.

I looked at her. I didn't love her. No matter how she was suffering. I think, I said.

What? she said again.

I think I don't love you, I said.

Just a figure of speech, of course. Try a little roughness, I said to myself. I'm always so gentle. But now she was looking at me. It wasn't getting through to her. That a man she'd met forty-eight hours earlier in a swimming pool, who, forty-eight hours later, is still there, at her bedside, could not love her. Or could love her. Well, especially not love her. Especially when she's in pain. And I wanted that to get through to her. I waited. And I saw this: she'd swallowed a healthy dose of pain. Of a different kind. One within my reach. So naive, I thought. You believed me.

I don't know, she said.

It was true, she didn't seem to know. Seemed lost. I collected myself a little.

I don't love you, I said, when you're like this.

Like what?

Changeable, I said.

It's because I'm in pain.

132

I don't like you to be in pain. What do I do to see her?

You go there. You can go there. First hallway on your left. There are arrows.

I found my way to the nursery. Asked to see Maude. I'll go and get her for you, said a neonatologist. Can I come with you? I said. We walked down a row of beds. Maude was wearing the world's smallest bracelet. With her name. I would have known her without it. Don't misunderstand me, I'm not bragging, after all I had nothing to do with it, but she was the most beautiful of them all. By far. Besides, the others weren't anything much, as babies go. Already that adult look, vaguely traveling-salesman-like. They were all the same.

No, I said. Leave her there. Maude wasn't crying in her little bed. I let her take my finger. The neonatologist went away. Maude, I breathed. Louder than the day before. No, not as loud. Clearer. So: Maude, I said. I can't stay long, your mother isn't well, she needs me. My name is Luc. Gavarine, I thought. I won't bring that up again, I said.

It was easy, smiling at her. With my eyes alone. Can I pick her up? I said. I turned around. The neonatologist had left the room. I picked up the child. She cried. Oh dear, I said. Don't cry, Maude. It's me, Luc. Come on, be quiet, I said, be quiet, people will think. Stop. Problem? said the neonatologist. Ah, I said. You're back. No, everything's fine, just fine. Well, she is crying, after all, the neonatologist said to me. I noticed, I said. Maybe she's hungry. Maybe so, said the neonatologist. Well, I'll let you look after her, I said. See you later, Maude, I said, bending over her. I kissed her on the nose, with the very tips of my lips. Gave her back. See you later, I said to the neonatologist.

I went back to Flore. She'd had some time to think. Everything OK? she said.

Yes, I said. She must have been hungry. She was crying.

133

Nothing much was resolved, to my surprise. No matter how sincere we tried to be, no matter how we tried to lie – well, her, mostly, I myself had nothing to hide, no merit, I'd even left my briefcase at the caverns, my one secret, at most, which in any case she already knew, not that she cared – we couldn't find a way out. There were tears, of course. Well, from Flore. Mostly from Flore. Not so much from me, as it happened. I'd seen worse. And yes, it helped when she cried. We moved forward. Physically. One toward the other. We needed help, both of us, we needed love, obviously, like anyone else, in the end, it was a very simple sort of problem. But not easy. Not for her. Apparently I wasn't the man who. I'm not the man you, I said. Yes, you are, she said. Yes. On the contrary. That On the contrary. Right, I finally said. Maybe I should come back tomorrow. You'll be older. Maybe you'll see things more clearly.

You idiot, she said.

I liked to make her feel relaxed when I was tense. That was my one little strength. And so we parted. It was better that way. I wouldn't have stayed another minute. We kissed. Chastely, all too. If you could find me a life preserver, she whispered. Excuse me? I said. An inflatable life preserver, to sit on. Because I can sit down, in theory. I'm not sick. But here I am lying down. Yes, I said, I see. And I hear. A life preserver, you say. What kind of life preserver? I don't know, she said. They told me a life preserver. Oh, I said. Where am I going to find one of those? I don't know, she said. They gave me a prescription. Let's see, I said. One life preserver, I read. That's it? What is this, a joke? Well, it could be, she said, that it's just an ordinary toy life preserver. Nothing unusual. That would surprise me, I said. I don't think they sell ordinary life preservers in pharmacies. That's true, she said. And on that minor mystery, we parted. Or almost. There was one other thing Flore wanted from me. Oh, no, she said, no, never mind, there's no need. I have my own. What are you talking about? I said. My blow-dryer, she said. They wanted me to get a blow-dryer because of my cut. I mean my stitches. To use a blow-dryer. Oh, I said. I didn't quite understand. Then I saw. Oh, I said, oh. What do you mean, oh? she said. You don't understand? The stitches. Yes, I said. Of course. Right. OK.

On the way back to the car, I thought. Not about us, no. About us I didn't want to think anymore. To wish us luck, at most. Like a third party, some sort of arbiter. Which is not what I was, obviously, far from it. No. I felt nothing. Nothing, and a great emptiness in my skull. And, behind me, ready to pounce, no. Not even that. No pain. None palpable, I mean. But a fear, nevertheless. Yes. Always now. Growing. Never gone. One single fear, without object. Vast. And a thought too, all the same. Absurd, niggling. No. Not all that niggling. I was thinking about that life preserver. And the hairdryer. The swimming supplies aspect. Sketchy, to be sure. Before and after. This oblique reminder of the pool struck me as curious. As if. As if what? I asked myself. Well, as if something weren't changing. Weren't evolving. From the swimming pool on. As if everything had come to a standstill after the swimming pool episode. Or had begun, rather. And ended. At the same time. As if there had been something in my life, in other words. But something behind me. Which, at this moment, yes, no doubt. But after this, no, nothing. Not even Maude. A lot of good her birth did. My own story went up to the swimming pool. After that, it wasn't my story anymore. It was other people's. Meanwhile, I said to myself, you go on clinging to it. And that's a mistake. That's what Flore was trying to tell me with her hairdryer and her life preserver.

Well, I said. This isn't helping anything. Stop talking nonsense, will you? Just keep going until you reach the car. Go back to the caverns. They're expecting you. And stop by a pharmacy on the way. That's a lot to do. A lot of things that people are expecting you to do. So do them. You should be able to see this is what comes next. That there's something that comes next. So come on, just go on, and stop imagining things. Anyway.

Oh, said the pharmacist. We can order one for you. But it won't be here until next week. I was double-parked, as on the way in. Maybe I could find one somewhere else, I said. You can always try, she said.

And so I did. Say, I said to myself, this time I'm going to try and parallel-park. I was beginning to feel at home behind the wheel. So I tried. Soon gave it up. Double-parked again. We can order you one, said the pharmacist, another woman. The number of women in that profession. But it won't be here before next week, she went on to say. Wait, I said. This life preserver, what's it like? What does it look like? It's just an ordinary toy life preserver, she said. So, I said, why do you sell them? Excuse me? she said. You're a pharmacy, I said. And you sell ordinary life preservers. Yes, she said, why? No reason, I said. Are they expensive? A little bit, she said. Do you know where there might be a variety store around here? I said. Are there any lakes nearby? Why yes, she said. Of course. Out by the caverns. But why? Why are you angry? No reason, I said, you know about the caverns? They're very well known around here, she said. I was disappointed. Anyway. Thanks, I said. And I headed toward the caverns. Found the arrow for the lake. Then the little store in the village near the lake. I studied the window display. Then I went in. Life preservers, I said to the shopkeeper. Do you have one without the duck? Without the duck? he said to me. Yes, I said. On the front. All your life preservers have a duck sticking out the front. Do you have any without? Oh, he said. You just want an ordinary life preserver? Yes, I said. I'll go see, he said.

136

He disappeared into the back. This is the only one I have left, he told me as he came out again, vaguely embarrassed. There's no duck sticking out the front of this one. You're right, I said. The duck was printed on. All around the upper half, many times duplicated. The underside was solid red. Fine, I said, this will do.

I gauged the diameter. I also checked for an airlock on the valve. Found one. I reached the caverns without mishap, reflecting that I'd learned at least one thing that day. I can drive, I said to myself. Undeniably, I have a talent.

I found the uncle at the front desk. You getting along? I said. No problems, he said. How about Jean? I said. I suppose he's down below? Yes, he told me. Oh, here he comes.

So? Jean said to me. Everything's fine, I said. Everything went fine. Except the stoplights. But that's coming along.

What about Flore?

She hurts a little. The episiotomy.

And the little one?

Maude's doing very well.

Here, things have been a bit slow, Jean told me. Roger's getting along just fine, though. Aren't you, Roger?

Obviously, said the uncle. Not much of a crowd.

No, said Jean. But all the same. Maybe it's me. How are you at climbing? he said to me. Stairs, I mean. You have an elevator in your building?

His breathing was heavier than ever. It frightened me. And now he was talking about my building. Really, I said to myself. What is it with these people? But no. I won't go further back than the swimming pool. Never. The swimming pool is my limit.

You want me to take over for you, I said.

What would you think of that?

Hope, in the eyes of a weary man. And a heavy one.

That would be fine, I said. Why not? And what would you be doing in the meantime?

I'll look after the front desk. The cashbox, that is. It's better that way, for the accounts. You see what I mean. And I'll give Roger his freedom.

I can stay, said Roger. I'm managing.

That's not the question, said Jean.

Fine, I intervened. But you'd have to explain it all for me. I don't know the first thing about this cavern of yours. I don't know anything about any caverns.

What can I tell you? said Jean. What would I do without you? But that can wait till tomorrow. Showing you around, I mean. Just now I can't. But tomorrow, yes. Before the tours. I'll lend you some boots.

Boots? I said.

Yes, he said. You haven't noticed I wear boots?

No, I said. Well, yes. I see.

It's wet down there.

What about the others? The visitors? The ones that don't have boots?

You'll have to warn them. You tell them before you set out. If you have boots, put them on now. The rest of you, don't try going down there in espadrilles. And bring a sweater. At the cave's deepest point, twenty-five meters, and you should emphasize the twenty-five, right, say it loud and clear, the temperature holds at a steady eleven to twelve degrees centigrade year-round. After the heat outside, you could easily catch a chill. So that's how you begin.

That sounds easy enough, I said.

After that, Jean told me, it becomes more technical.

We got up at eight o'clock. Ate breakfast. Bathed, then dressed. Booted, I followed in Jean's footsteps toward the entrance. I'd never been near the fence before. Jean produced a key, opened the gate. We continued toward the stairway. The walls of rock before us green and leafy. Then greener and greener, and mossy, as we descended. Covered with something like ferns. Scolopendria, Jean said. Should I tell them that? I asked. No, said Jean, nobody cares about the plant life. They're here for the rocks. I'm just telling you. That's nice of you, I said.

On the other hand, said Jean, you should explain to them where they are. What it is they're going into. This is a swallow. Which is to say a hole in the earth. Created by a subsidence, of course. Tell them that. Ladies and gentlemen, we now find ourselves in a swallow.

We passed through a second door, this one solid. A second key. The stairway grew damp. Then wet. I could feel the cold. Following behind Jean, I raised my head. My gaze climbed the wall. The light at the top was dazzling. Couldn't reach us here. But, seen from below, made the patch of sky vibrate before your eyes. The stairway turned a corner. Farther on, lower down, I could see a fallen boulder half blocking the entrance to a gallery. We continued our advance through the murky light. Spotlights brought out niches, defined contrasts, emphasized hues. The rocks oozed water. Reliefs leapt out, not unlike what I'd seen on the posters in the office. But not as real. Jean had revealed them by switching on a series of lights, throwing a set of little levers in a cupboard on the way down. You remember, naturally, he said to me, and I noticed the curious lack of reso-

139

nance in his voice, the difference between a stalactite, but I cut him off. Really now, I said. Whatever you do, don't bring that up, he told me, you don't want to turn anyone off, right? Obviously, I said. You can trust me. You may, Jean said again, now admire the beauty of the formations, their exquisite delicacy, that you can say, if you must, but I'm getting ahead of myself, first you have to show them the gallery. That's where you really begin.

We were entering an empty space, roughly circular, slightly uphill from the gallery, whose threshold alone was lit amid the gloom. Visitors, by my estimation, would be forced to stoop ever so slightly as they passed through. Flared on both sides, the fallen rock made a bottleneck, in coalition with the wall, into whose depths the gaze penetrated with difficulty, soon encountering an almost perfectly black darkness edged with yellow by a distant spotlight. The sound of dripping water could be heard in the distance.

On the whole, then, it was dark, and in the final analysis none too well lit. From time to time I looked at my feet. We were walking in water. Jean was now beginning the tour in earnest, and, as agreed, I took notes. I'd brought a little notebook with me. Sometimes I asked him to repeat. Column, he said. Very simply. Gateway. Wait, I said, what's that? Am I talking too fast? he said. No, I said. You're walking too fast. I didn't have time to see.

We stopped. I asked him to back up. I wanted to step back for a look. It's impressive, I said. You like it? he said. That's not the word, I said. I think it's. You'll have to work on your patter, he said. You see there, those are the guardians. Those two stalagmites. The guardians of the gateway. If there are children, for instance, you can say, and now, if there are any children present (act as if you hadn't seen them, in the dark), children, then, you say, who want to ask the guardians' permission to pass through the gateway, well. Just as a joke, you see. To keep it light. That breaks things up a bit.

Yes, I said. Can we go back a little?

What's that? What do you want to see?

The mammoth tusk, I said. But I don't want to see it. I want you to tell me again. What it is we're seeing.

We turned around. There, said Jean. On your left, you will notice a black vertical line. And cutting across that line, a sort of white stick. Can everyone see that? Get closer, go on, don't be afraid. Yes, right there. What that is, is a mammoth tusk. It's been dated to three hundred thousand years ago. Let me remind you that archeologists have unearthed a great variety of bones in this cavern, a small sampling of which you can inspect in our little museum behind the office. The caverns functioned as a natural animal trap. Now, he went on to say, whispering, oddly, don't go on too long about the tusk. It's up to them to see it. They see what they want to see, in the end. Emphasize the rock, always. And remind them that not the slightest trace of human presence has ever been found here. It's strange, but they like that. It impresses them. And furthermore it's true. OK?

Yes, I said. OK.

I wrote quickly. Not everything. We came back to the gateway. Passed through. Made our way around a number of suggestive forms. An erect member, a breast. A white, round breast, man-sized, vertical. I touched it. I'm making myself at home, I said. Of course, said Jean. But don't touch anything in front of the others, right? Obviously, I said.

We continued toward the exit, with Jean pursuing his commentary. The ground sloped upward, imperceptibly, with an abrupt flight of steps grafted onto the rock. A hand-painted sign reminded the visitors not to forget the guide. Oh, said Jean. While I'm thinking about it. You should ask for tips. Just to make it lifelike. Unless, he said to me. You do want me to pay you?

I've lost my job, I said.

No, he said. That's impossible.

Yes, I said, it happens. It happens to me. But I.

There's a fixed salary, Jean told me. It's not much, but with tips you get close to minimum wage. A little less. The real problem is that we close down at the end of October. There's nothing going on here in the winter. And then there's the guide. It's her job. You'll have to find something else.

In the meantime, I said.

In the meantime, of course. I'm just thinking about Maude. It's going to be tight.

I know, I said. But it's no big deal. I'm not her father.

We were emerging into the clearing, through a door housed in a little building at some distance from the rest and built, I realized as I turned around, for that solitary purpose. To house a door. It was the door's house, nothing more than that, a little house for it alone. With a huge basement, of course. I liked that. A false house.

I don't quite understand, said Jean.

Maude, I said. I'm not her father. I only met Flore the day before yesterday.

He put his hand to his mouth, as old women sometimes do. You can't make that kind of thing up.

That's impossible, he said again.

Yes, it's true, I said. At the swimming pool.

Oh, he said.

He seemed to understand. Because of the pool. To him, visibly, it was different at the pool. Such things could be, at the

142

pool. One could not be the father. In a movie, in a movie the-
ater, there I don't know.

But then the father, he said. After all. The guy.

I don't know, I said.

But of course, he said.

He was thinking to himself. That seemed better to me.

But of course, he went on, that's not really the problem.

I couldn't have agreed more. We complemented each other. I
added a further observation: The problem is that I'm not sure
Flore loves me. That's the real problem.

I don't know her very well, Jean told me. She's only my sister.

Well, I said, I know my sister quite well.

Oh really?

But I'm not going to tell you about my sister now, I said. You
tell me about yours instead.

She's a good person, said Jean. I like her. But tell me you two
have at least talked a little.

We've talked a bit, I said, but I've never. I can't be sure that.

Well, what the hell are you doing here, then? he said to me.
What did you think would happen?

I didn't think at all, I said. I've had it with thinking. I came.
She was willing to have me come.

She asked you to?

I'm not sure anymore.

Oh, said Jean, this is all very troubling.

I didn't mean to upset you, I said.

No, no, he said. I'm not really upset. It's your business. It's just
Flore.

How do you mean?

She'll never understand why I'm keeping you here. If she
doesn't love you.

Deep down, I said, even that's not certain. Maybe she does
love me. Or will love me. And of course I love her.

That touched him. Cast him into a deep reverie too. From which he emerged, after the requisite silence, as if just awakened. Abruptly.

Just like that? he said. In two days?

No, I said. I already loved her, at the pool.

Yes, he said. (He seemed pensive again, but less so, far less.) They say that can happen. And of course I wasn't there, was I?

You can trust me, I said. Already at the pool.

I could see that I had there, with the pool, or with the word pool, I'm not sure which, a powerful argument. Maybe he was sensitive to words like that; maybe certain words set something off inside him. You never know with people.

Right, he said to me. Well, we'll just assume.

What do you mean, I said, assume?

You'll stay here. And help me with the caverns. And we'll wait.

Wait for what?

You have another suggestion?

He was losing his patience. This was the first time. Like his sister. Right. Fine.

No, I said, that doesn't sound too bad. It seems reasonable. A reasonable solution. Yes.

I led my first tour that afternoon. A small group, seven people, specifically two couples and their children, who ran off in all directions, yelled, put their hands everywhere, tried to climb on everything, and Jean had never touched on the problem of maintaining discipline. I improvised. Let's quiet down now, I said. We don't touch the formations. And we don't shout. We're deep underground here, and we can't be sure we'll ever find our way out. I'm only kidding, I whispered to the parents. For here, I resumed aloud, the slightest jolt can have repercussions. Serious repercussions. That's why, I added, lowering my voice a little, I avoid speaking too loudly. Otherwise, up above, crack. Things fall. Look. Those pointed things. Stalactites, yes. We are now standing in a veritable deathtrap for wild animals.

A little more elaborate than what Jean had told me, of course, but I succeeded in restoring order. The children kept quiet. Stopped running around. I showed them the mammoth tusk. No hard feelings. For the tour proper I fell back on Jean's version. I'd studied the brochure as well. I like this place, I said to the adults when it came time to wind things up. It's sort of my private domain. So I feel protective toward it. You understand. Don't forget the guide.

They looked through their pockets. I held out my hand. We emerged into the sunlight. I let them go on ahead of me toward the clearing, while I stayed behind facing the door. I loved that little building, made to house nothing. Its sloping roof, one-sided. The caverns below, undetectable. I thought about my briefcase. I used to carry emptiness around with me. Now I walked around inside it. I'm making progress, I said to myself, I'm making progress.

Mind you, I was no dupe. I knew that on the whole everything was screwed, that no miracle would occur. Flore wouldn't be any more in love with me when she got out of the hospital. But I hung on. To what I didn't know, but to whom I did. To Jean. He comforted me. His innocence. I wanted to believe him. Not that he'd said much of anything, of course. But that didn't matter. I had faith in him. As soon as he did say something, I would believe him. And even if he never did. I was there. Just like home. Because that he had said to me, and of course I was having some difficulty believing it. But I wanted to. In the end, I said to myself, it's all a matter of desire. My desire is to stay here. I wanted to be happy here. Until it all falls apart.

The next day I went back to the hospital. I had an accident. A crumpled fender, nothing more. But I was upset. I didn't want to wear out my welcome. Jean only had one car.

I kissed Flore briefly, held out the life preserver. She protested. You don't think it's funny? I said. Not really, she said. I understand, I said.

And it's true, I did understand. I would have been reluctant to sit on that life preserver myself. Humbly, I recognized my misjudgment: the thought of sitting on ducks would not be enough to let her laugh this off. Even without the ducks, there was nothing terribly amusing about it. The same could be said of the atmosphere in the room. I found myself asking Flore if I was disturbing her. No, she told me. In any case, I didn't really want to see her. I wanted to be with her. And I wasn't. I went to see Maude.

With her it was different. She recognized me. Took my finger. I could see something was happening there. This child, I said to myself. She's not my doing, fine. But she's not my invention, either. She exists.

I wasn't long at the hospital. I didn't really feel like staying with Maude either. In the end, Maude without her mother wasn't quite what I wanted. Since she was born, I realized I'd always needed a mother, for her sake. And I still did. I still felt the same need. And need, I said to myself, is a little like desire; you have to give it time. So let's wait.

I went back to the caverns. Gave Jean an update. Tomorrow, I said, you can go and see for yourself. You have every right to see her. You can call your uncle again for the desk.

We understood each other like that. I asked Jean, by the way, if by chance Flore might know anyone. Anyone else. Or if he did. There was never anyone at the hospital. Didn't I hear you mention a family? I asked.

You must not have been listening, he said. They're all dead.

Oh, I said.

It's true, my mind must have been on other things. I didn't go on to grill him about friends, possible friends. I was afraid they might be dead too. Insofar as they were family.

That evening we had dinner with the waitress. She'd stayed behind at Jean's invitation. She was like family, in a way. So it seemed to me. I'd never seen them talking together, just the two of them, but neither was I always there to see everything. Between courses, she dealt with the dishes. Never really present at the table, then, but talkative. She seemed to get along well with him. I began to wonder if, possibly, but I preferred not to venture into that domain. The ground was not entirely solid there. Nevertheless, when the cheese course rolled around, I wouldn't swear to it, but it seemed to me that in the vicinity of the plate, in the context of a knife passed from one to the other, their hands brushed. I soon suspected a long history to their reserve, which that evening looked suspiciously like determination, or even doggedness. That Jean was reserved behind his

147

air of not being so, that I knew, but in the density of their avoid-
ance, I sensed something excessive. Their conversation, too
resolutely light, sometimes meandering, with occasional for-
ays into international affairs that fooled no one, was not slow to
reveal, as the wine took hold, the skeleton that held it earth-
bound. Suzanne, said Jean, at one anodyne moment, or which
seemed anodyne to me. This was the first time he'd spoken the
waitress's name in my presence, and I thought that was it. It
nearly was. Luc, he added. From what followed, I understood
that he intended to include me in their after-dinner plans, and
at first I assumed this was purely a formality, so that I might act
as a buffer between their twin modesties, but no, or not only.
Jean, I later realized, genuinely wanted to include me. I would
have to adopt an unfailingly self-effacing character for the occasion, which was frankly not my cup of tea, but I readily con-
sented to the sacrifice.

He took us to the museum. Let us not forget that Jean had a
museum of his own, next to the office. We viewed the bones.
Despite her solid grounding in the social niceties, and despite
the great rigor of her opinions – essentially in line with the
Fourth International, albeit with certain nuances that she'd
outlined at dinner, hammering the tabletop with her delicate
fist – Suzanne was still quite young, and wine induced in her a
sort of tendency to list. She supported herself against the glass
tops of the microfauna cases. Birds, amphibians, rodents, Jean
pointed out, holding her up by the armpits. Go look over there,
he said to me. The radius. The giant radius. We'll catch up with
you. I can hold her by myself.

It was a very nice radius, from a woolly rhinoceros, which
eventually we all contemplated together, slumped over the display case. You've never seen the museum before? Jean said to
me. You never came in here?

148

Not that he really suspected me. But I reassured him all the same. I'd never undertaken anything here without his explicit authorization. More than anything, what I wanted was to be of use to him. To follow his instructions. Nothing more. But I was glad to be shown the museum. Now I'd seen everything there was to see, at the caverns.

You're my friend, he told me.

This was a bit much. He'd had a few. But I didn't tell him so. It takes longer than that to build a friendship, I thought. To move beyond the utilitarian. Which was what I wanted, of course. To be comfortable with him, without self-interest. But my need for him still felt like a captive need. I still saw him as a guide. I'd already entered onto it, but I still couldn't see the path ahead all that clearly.

He, on the other hand, needed me to an extent that I began to grasp more clearly that evening. We drank a bit more after we left the museum. Finally he made a gesture in Suzanne's direction. A sort of overt grazing of her person. She melted. Discreetly, but she melted. Right in front of me. I felt a slight desire to die, at that moment, but it went away. At least I hadn't been left out. And I didn't suspect Jean of exhibitionist tendencies. Rather, I think he wanted me there as a witness. I couldn't help but sense that he was testing the waters, in that domain.

The next day, as agreed, I didn't go and see Flore. Or Maude. I was somewhat distressed that it had come to this, to having to do without them, but in the end it didn't really hurt me. Or no longer hurt me. I'd made up my mind to wait for them. I spent the day oscillating between the caverns and the front desk, talking with the uncle. One who was spared. I asked him about the family, and he recounted the hecatomb. Cursorily. None of that aggrieved him much anymore. Too old. Was fond of Jean and wished he would call on him more often. Confessed that,

149

outside of his municipal activities, which took up 50 percent of his time, he didn't know quite what to do with himself. Maybe that will take care of itself, I said. They need you here. I see it every day. What about Flore? I added. You haven't been to see her? She's your niece, isn't she?

He made a gesture. Not dismissive, no. As if to say there was no need. That, in spite of his age, he had time. That the two of them would come to the caverns. In a few days. And he would be there. If everything went as it should. And then. He took a package from beneath the table. A large package, gift-wrapped, cubical. You see, he said to me. I've got it all planned out.

The next day I went to the hospital. This was beginning to feel like a routine. Except where Maude was concerned. I talked to her more this time, and she seemed to be listening. That was encouraging. Your mother, I said. Then I stopped talking. I knew I had to be very careful, pedagogically speaking. To Flore I said only that I understood. That it was over, between us. That it had been nice, all the same. Wait, she said. I quivered, but not much. I put myself on alert.

Everything's going fine, she told me. And I'm sick of lying here hurting. I'm coming home tomorrow.

I waited. That wasn't enough. Just because she was coming home tomorrow. Even if I was at the caverns, we wouldn't be reunited. Not necessarily. I'd told her I was at the caverns for now. Helping Jean. And Jean, no doubt, had told her too. But living with me, obviously. That was something else entirely.

I'm going home to my brother's tomorrow, she said. With Maude.

I waited some more. She spoke slowly.

I've been thinking, she said. I think you're right.

Well, I said to myself. There we are. She's going to ask Jean to send me away. But maybe Jean. I'm not gone yet. I won't dig in my heels, fine. But let her at least tell me. To go away. Just let her tell me that. I'm used to it.

All the same, I was thinking of Maude, all that. What a mess. But then maybe that will be the depths, I told myself. The depths of pain, remember? That's what you were looking for, isn't it? At one point. Which seems so far away now. Maybe she's about to give you the chance. That chance.

You're right, she told me, I don't love you.

Oh, I said to myself, here it comes. Although I can't really imagine what she could say that would be worse than this. Yes, this must be it. I must be there now. That's it. Yes. Of course. Just in case, I took a seat.

But, she told me, I know you won't understand this.

I don't think understanding really enters into it, I said. Into these things.

I felt weary, more than I usually do, when I feel weary.

I'd like you to stay, she said.

I stood up.

Wait, I said. Can you say that again?

In the same tone of voice? she said.

Yes, I said.

I'd like you to stay, she said.

It was the same tone of voice. A little graver. That will do, I said to myself. Oh, I said to her. Oh, now. You can't.

I don't want you to take it too well, she said.

Oh yes, I said, oh yes.

Because as far as I'm concerned the whole arrangement sort of leaves me cold, she said, you understand. Since I don't love you.

You might come to love me, I said.

That would surprise me, she said.

Since I love you, I said.

Yes, she said. It's going to be difficult, between you and me.

You're forgetting Maude, I said.

No, she said. That's part of it too.

Especially if her father comes back, I said.

He won't come back.

You never know, I said. It's best to expect the worst. Don't reassure me too much. That's not exactly what I want from you.

Luc, she said.

Yes?

She took my hand.

Nothing, she said. I just hope you'll be a little more sensible with Maude.

The next day I went to pick them up at the hospital. Jean let me go, in spite of his concerns. I explained that, for me, for Flore, for Maude, especially, this was no time for an accident. Just because I'd crumpled one of his fenders. I'm not afraid anymore, now, I said to him. He believed me. I was touched by his confidence.

At the hospital we made our farewells to the staff. I felt so full of love that day, I would gladly have taken them all home with us. I'm exaggerating. But I did ask for news of the nurse in the basement. No one knew what I was talking about. It was a big hospital, but still. She fell down, I told them. Fainted in the basement. No?

No. I was particularly eager to say hello to the midwife. I talked to her about the intern. Together we considered the procedures for making a complaint. She was a great help to us, I said to Flore as we left. She assented. Can you walk? I asked her. It's OK, she said. I asked her another question, any question. She acquiesced again. But I didn't push my luck. I asked her nothing more. I think she needed quiet. Time to get used to things. I carried Maude for her. Flore sat down in the back seat, on her life preserver, with the baby carrier next to her. Strapped down, all the same. I insisted.

We arrived at the caverns without mishap. I drove slowly, maybe a little too slowly. Flore expressed some dismay on that point. I offered to make it fast. That was the one time all day that she failed to agree with me. It warmed me.

Jean was waiting for us at the caverns. The uncle was there as well, and young Suzanne, all three standing in front of the office. They weren't alone. There was a group waiting patiently in the background. When we arrived, they came and joined the trio. Hello! someone shouted in English. A party of British visitors. They waved at us. Awaiting us, them too. Jean had clearly let them in on the secret. He wanted to make a party of it. Everyone embraced. Hello! I said. I shook hands. Very pale, Flore passed from one breast to the next, relinquished Maude to the uncle. The child was circulated. Let's have a drink, said Jean.

We gathered on the terrace. Suzanne served. The British grew expansive. They thought the place delightful. The people. Liqueurs were poured. In a while, said Jean, you really will go and see the caverns. He was speaking French. Happily, the British too. Especially one of them. We have time, he said. This is our holiday. Ours too, said Jean. This is a special day. He tried to catch Suzanne's eye. Caught it. Laughed. I smiled. I was watching them out of the corner of my eye. It's taking shape, I said to myself, my left elbow occupied by Maude. I rocked her, distractedly. She cried. Flore, I said. She was gazing into the distance, listening to who knows what. What voices. Yes, she said. She took the child. She carried her inside, toward the bar. Sat down on a chair. I could see them from where I was sitting. Applying themselves, the pair of them. There we are, I said to myself. There we are. Right, said Jean. Now, how about another drink for the rest of us too? It's depressing, looking at all these empty glasses.

Suzanne served us again. She left the bottles on the table. We poured ourselves some more. The British could hardly contain themselves now. If this keeps up, I said to myself, they'll be singing soon. Right, said Jean. How about we go see the caverns? All together. Let's get them moving a little, he whispered to me. A little fresh air. OK, we're right behind you, the Englishman declared. You have boots? I said to him.

154

We started down the terrace steps. Jean stumbled. I caught him. Well, I said. You can lead the tour, he told me. Obviously, I said. Nothing has to change.

I took charge of the group. We arrived at the gate. To the caverns. Wait, I said. I looked through my pockets. How stupid of me, I said. I forgot the keys. Don't move. I'll be right back.

I headed toward the office. Near the table, on the wall, I found the keys. Hanging on their nail. I took them down. Went out again. Strolled back to the group. Close-knit. Unsteady. Some of them clinging to others. Here we are, I said. (I showed them the keys.) Just takes a moment. Now we can go on.